GHOSTLY GRAPHIC ADVENTURES

DODGING DANGER ON THE DARTMOUTH

Written by Baron Specter
Illustrated by Dustin Evans

magic wagon

visit us at www.abdopublishing.com

Published by Magic Wagon, a division of the ABDO Group, 8000 West 78th Street, Edina, Minnesota 55439. Copyright © 2011 by Abdo Consulting Group, Inc. International copyrights reserved in all countries. All rights reserved. No part of this book may be reproduced in any form without written permission from the publisher.

Graphic Planet™ is a trademark and logo of Magic Wagon.

Printed in the United States of America, North Mankato, Minnesota.
032010
092010
♻This book contains at least 10% recycled materials.

Written by Baron Specter
Illustrated by Dustin Evans
Lettered and designed by Ardden Entertainment LLC
Edited by Stephanie Hedlund and Rochelle Baltzer
Cover art by Dustin Evans
Cover design by Ardden Entertainment LLC

Library of Congress Cataloging-in-Publication Data

Specter, Baron, 1957-
   The first adventure : dodging danger on the Dartmouth / by Baron Specter; illustrated by Dustin Evans.
      p. cm. -- (Ghostly graphic adventures)
   Summary: While on a school field trip, Joey and Tank encounter a ghostly captain aboard a historical ship and, upon their return that night, travel through time and become involved in the Boston Tea Party.
   ISBN 978-1-60270-770-2
  1. Graphic novels. [1. Graphic novels. 2. Ghosts--Fiction. 3. Time travel--Fiction. 4. Boston Tea Party, 1773--Fiction. 5. Boston (Mass.)--History--Colonial period, ca. 1600-1775--Fiction. 6. Boston (Mass.)--Fiction.] I. Evans, Dustin, 1982- ill. II. Title. III. Title: Dodging danger on the Dartmouth.
   PZ7.7.S648Fir 2010
   741.5'973--dc22
                              2009052721

TABLE OF CONTENTS

OUR HEROES AND VILLAINS

Joey DeAngelo
New Kid and Our Hero

Gil
Classmate and Sometimes Villain

Captain Hall
Our Villain

Tank
Classmate and Sometimes Villain

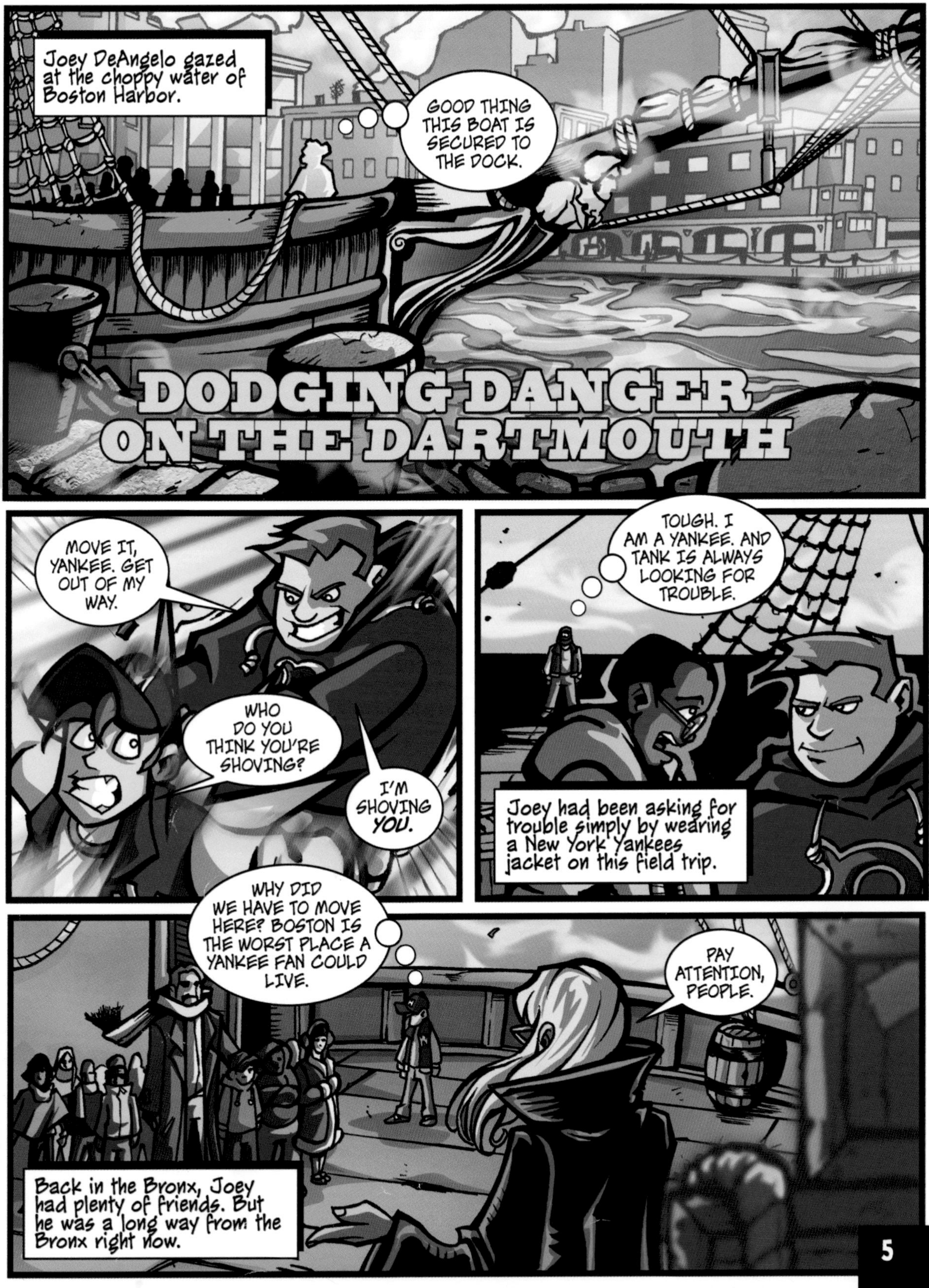

Joey DeAngelo gazed at the choppy water of Boston Harbor.
GOOD THING THIS BOAT IS SECURED TO THE DOCK.
DODGING DANGER ON THE DARTMOUTH
MOVE IT, YANKEE. GET OUT OF MY WAY.
WHO DO YOU THINK YOU'RE SHOVING?
I'M SHOVING *YOU*.
TOUGH. I AM A YANKEE. AND TANK IS ALWAYS LOOKING FOR TROUBLE.
Joey had been asking for trouble simply by wearing a New York Yankees jacket on this field trip.
WHY DID WE HAVE TO MOVE HERE? BOSTON IS THE WORST PLACE A YANKEE FAN COULD LIVE.
PAY ATTENTION, PEOPLE.
Back in the Bronx, Joey had plenty of friends. But he was a long way from the Bronx right now.

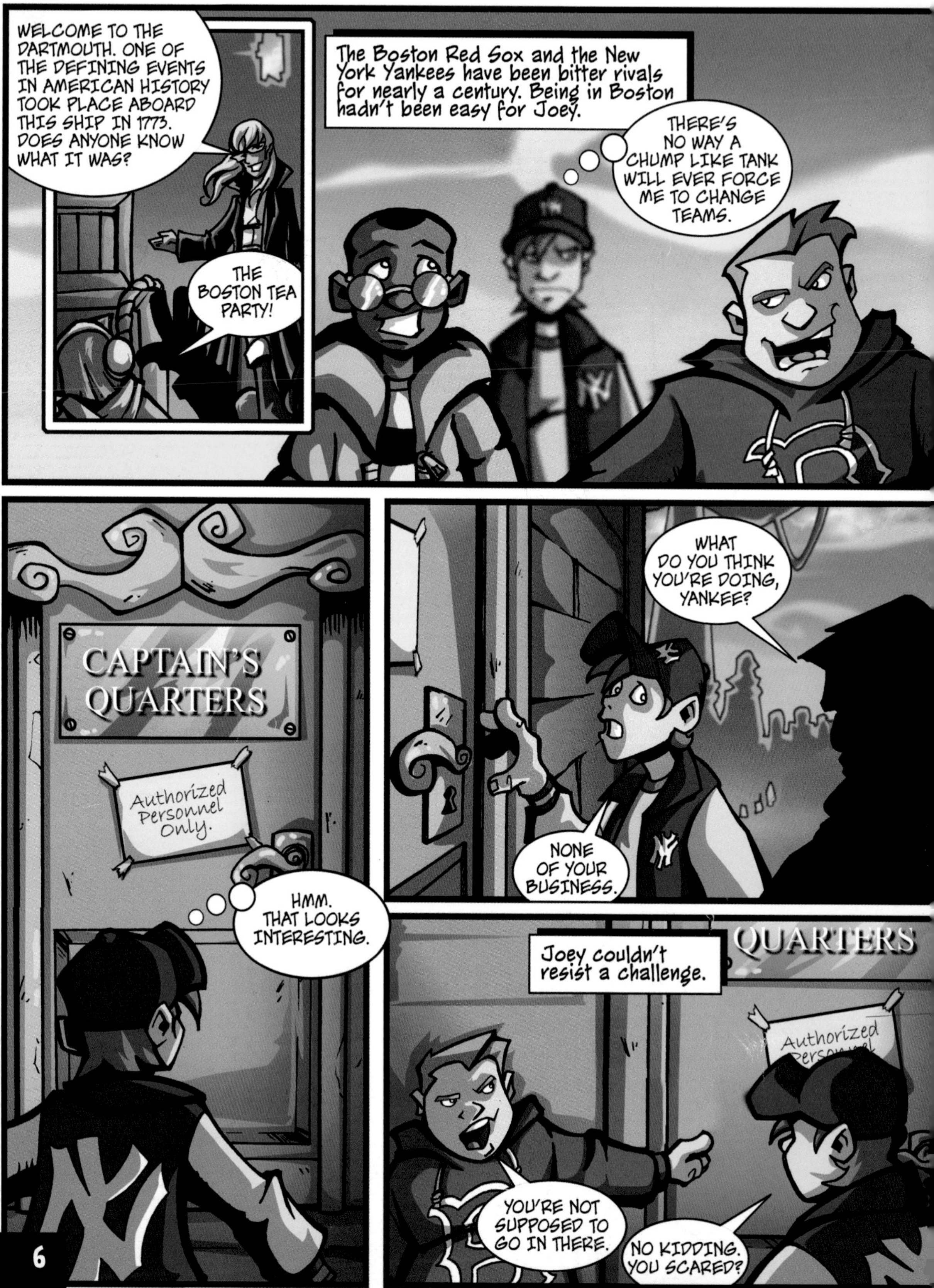

WELCOME TO THE DARTMOUTH. ONE OF THE DEFINING EVENTS IN AMERICAN HISTORY TOOK PLACE ABOARD THIS SHIP IN 1773. DOES ANYONE KNOW WHAT IT WAS?
THE BOSTON TEA PARTY!
The Boston Red Sox and the New York Yankees have been bitter rivals for nearly a century. Being in Boston hadn't been easy for Joey.
THERE'S NO WAY A CHUMP LIKE TANK WILL EVER FORCE ME TO CHANGE TEAMS.
CAPTAIN'S QUARTERS
Authorized Personnel Only.
HMM. THAT LOOKS INTERESTING.
WHAT DO YOU THINK YOU'RE DOING, YANKEE?
NONE OF YOUR BUSINESS.
QUARTERS
Joey couldn't resist a challenge.
Authorized
YOU'RE NOT SUPPOSED TO GO IN THERE.
NO KIDDING. YOU SCARED?

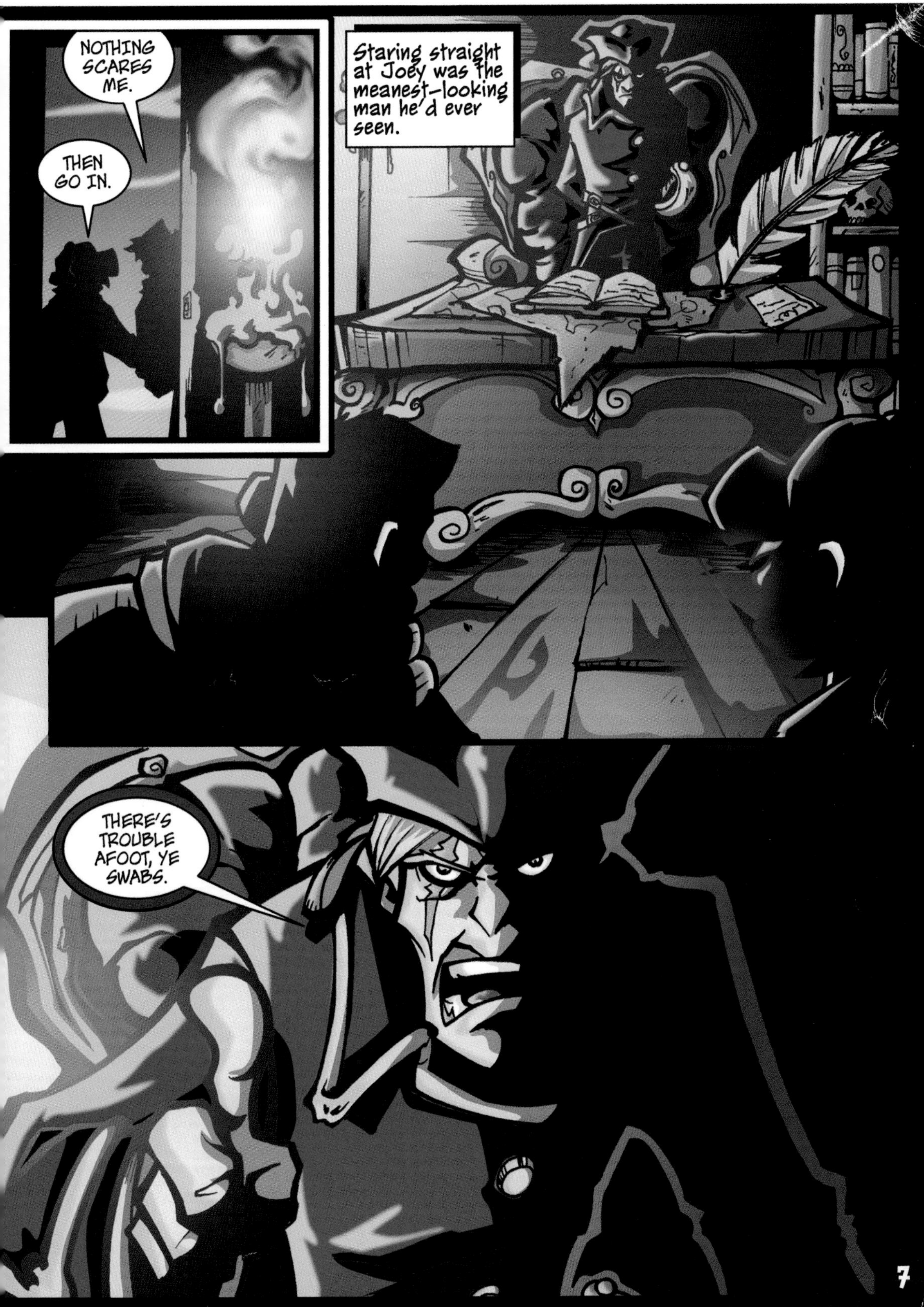
NOTHING SCARES ME.
THEN GO IN.
Staring straight at Joey was the meanest-looking man he'd ever seen.
THERE'S TROUBLE AFOOT, YE SWABS.

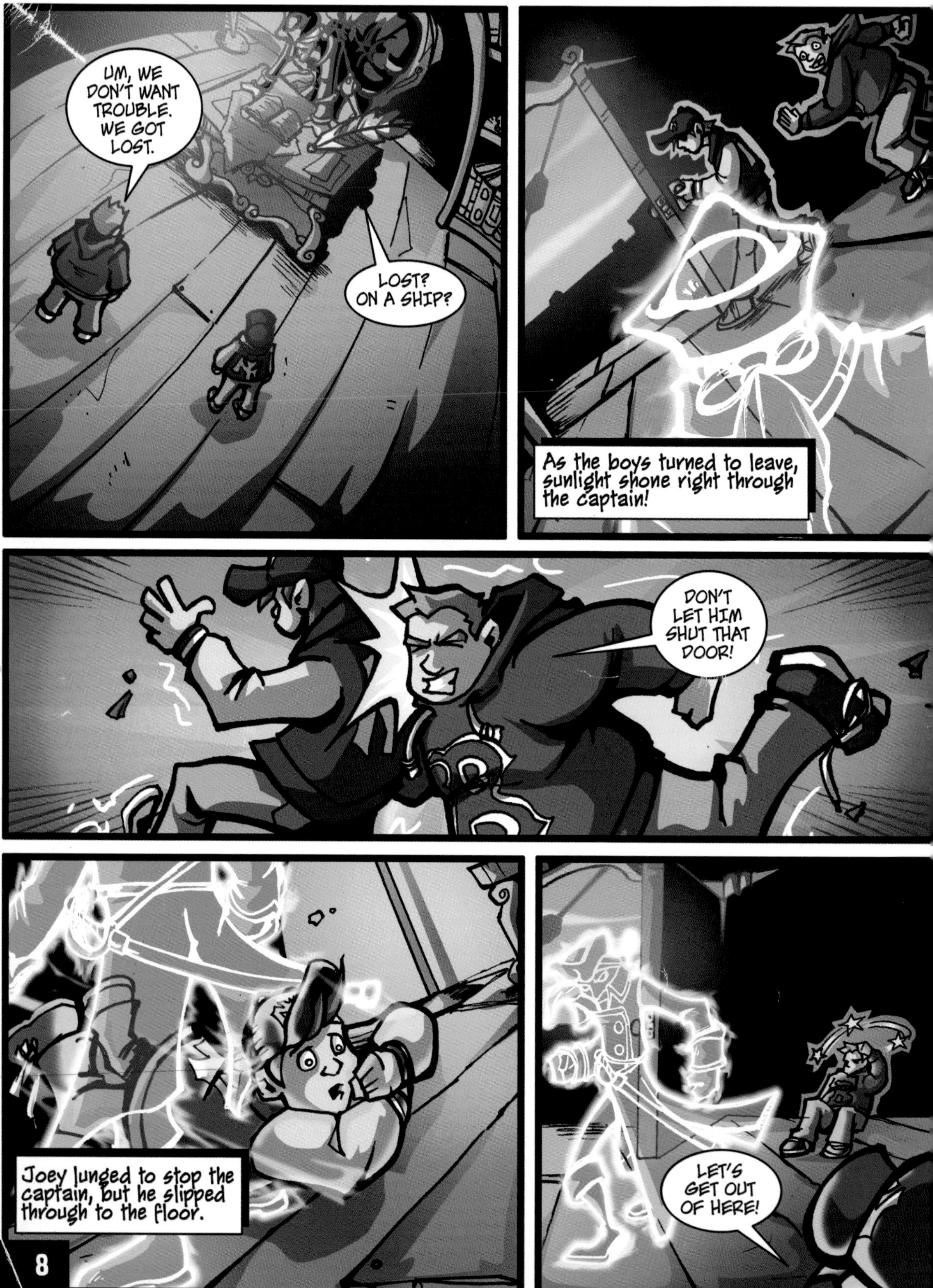
UM, WE DON'T WANT TROUBLE. WE GOT LOST.
LOST? ON A SHIP?
As the boys turned to leave, sunlight shone right through the captain!
DON'T LET HIM SHUT THAT DOOR!
Joey lunged to stop the captain, but he slipped through to the floor.
LET'S GET OUT OF HERE!

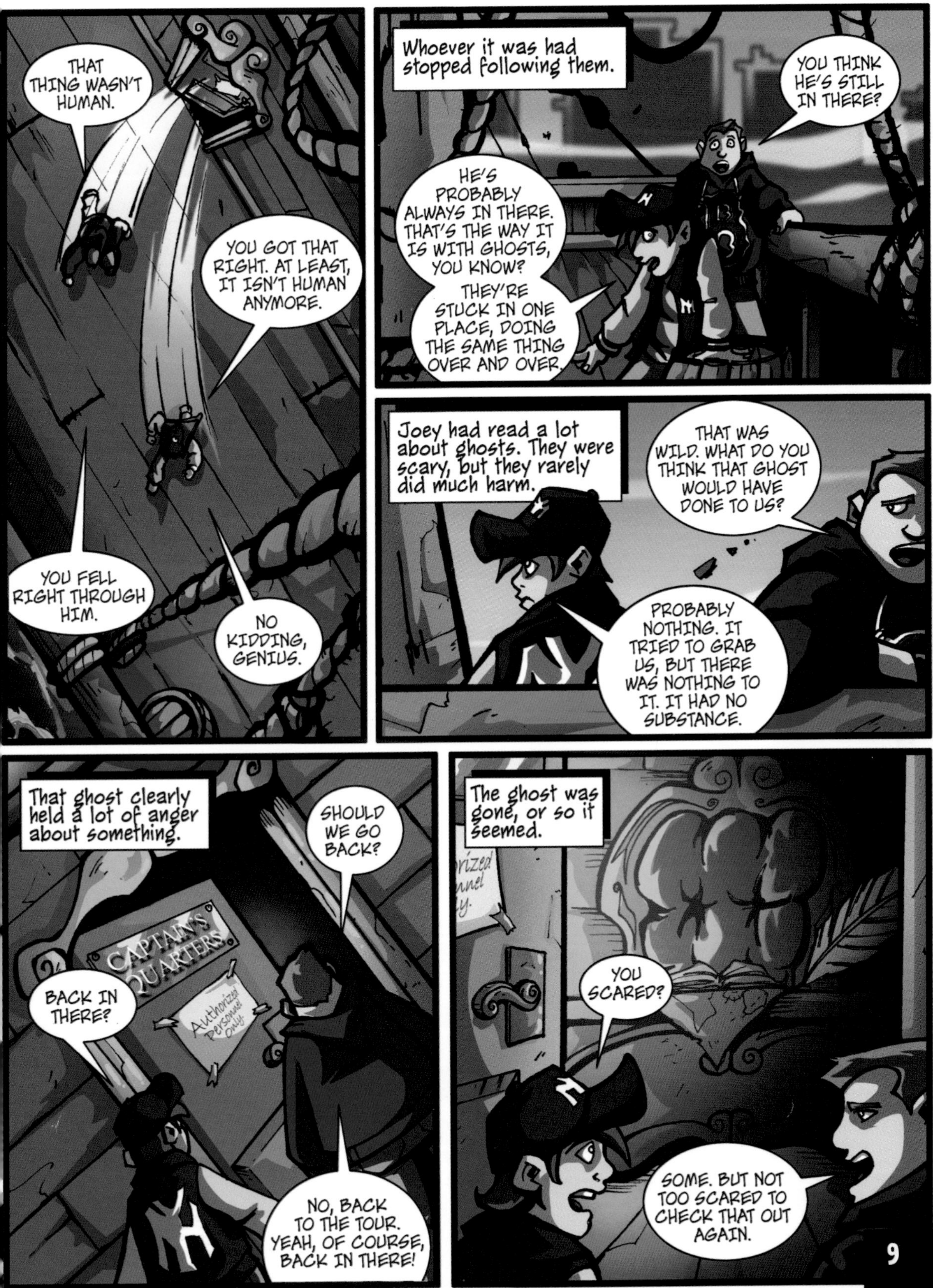
THAT THING WASN'T HUMAN.
YOU GOT THAT RIGHT. AT LEAST, IT ISN'T HUMAN ANYMORE.
YOU FELL RIGHT THROUGH HIM.
NO KIDDING, GENIUS.
Whoever it was had stopped following them.
YOU THINK HE'S STILL IN THERE?
HE'S PROBABLY ALWAYS IN THERE. THAT'S THE WAY IT IS WITH GHOSTS, YOU KNOW?
THEY'RE STUCK IN ONE PLACE, DOING THE SAME THING OVER AND OVER.
Joey had read a lot about ghosts. They were scary, but they rarely did much harm.
THAT WAS WILD. WHAT DO YOU THINK THAT GHOST WOULD HAVE DONE TO US?
PROBABLY NOTHING. IT TRIED TO GRAB US, BUT THERE WAS NOTHING TO IT. IT HAD NO SUBSTANCE.
That ghost clearly held a lot of anger about something.
SHOULD WE GO BACK?
CAPTAIN'S QUARTERS
Authorized Personnel Only
BACK IN THERE?
NO, BACK TO THE TOUR. YEAH, OF COURSE, BACK IN THERE!
The ghost was gone, or so it seemed.
YOU SCARED?
SOME. BUT NOT TOO SCARED TO CHECK THAT OUT AGAIN.

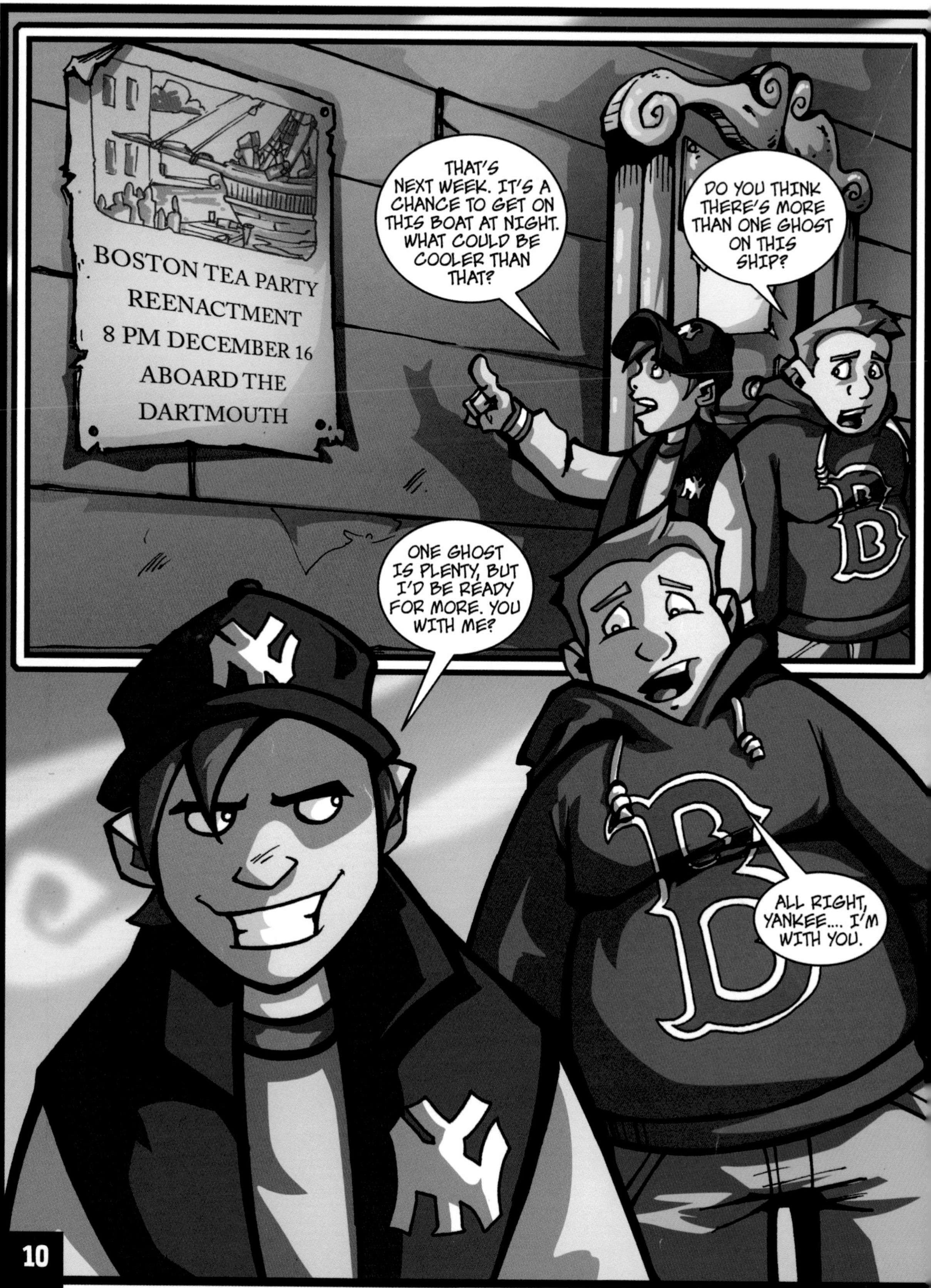
BOSTON TEA PARTY REENACTMENT 8 PM DECEMBER 16 ABOARD THE DARTMOUTH
THAT'S NEXT WEEK. IT'S A CHANCE TO GET ON THIS BOAT AT NIGHT. WHAT COULD BE COOLER THAN THAT?
DO YOU THINK THERE'S MORE THAN ONE GHOST ON THIS SHIP?
ONE GHOST IS PLENTY, BUT I'D BE READY FOR MORE. YOU WITH ME?
ALL RIGHT, YANKEE.... I'M WITH YOU.

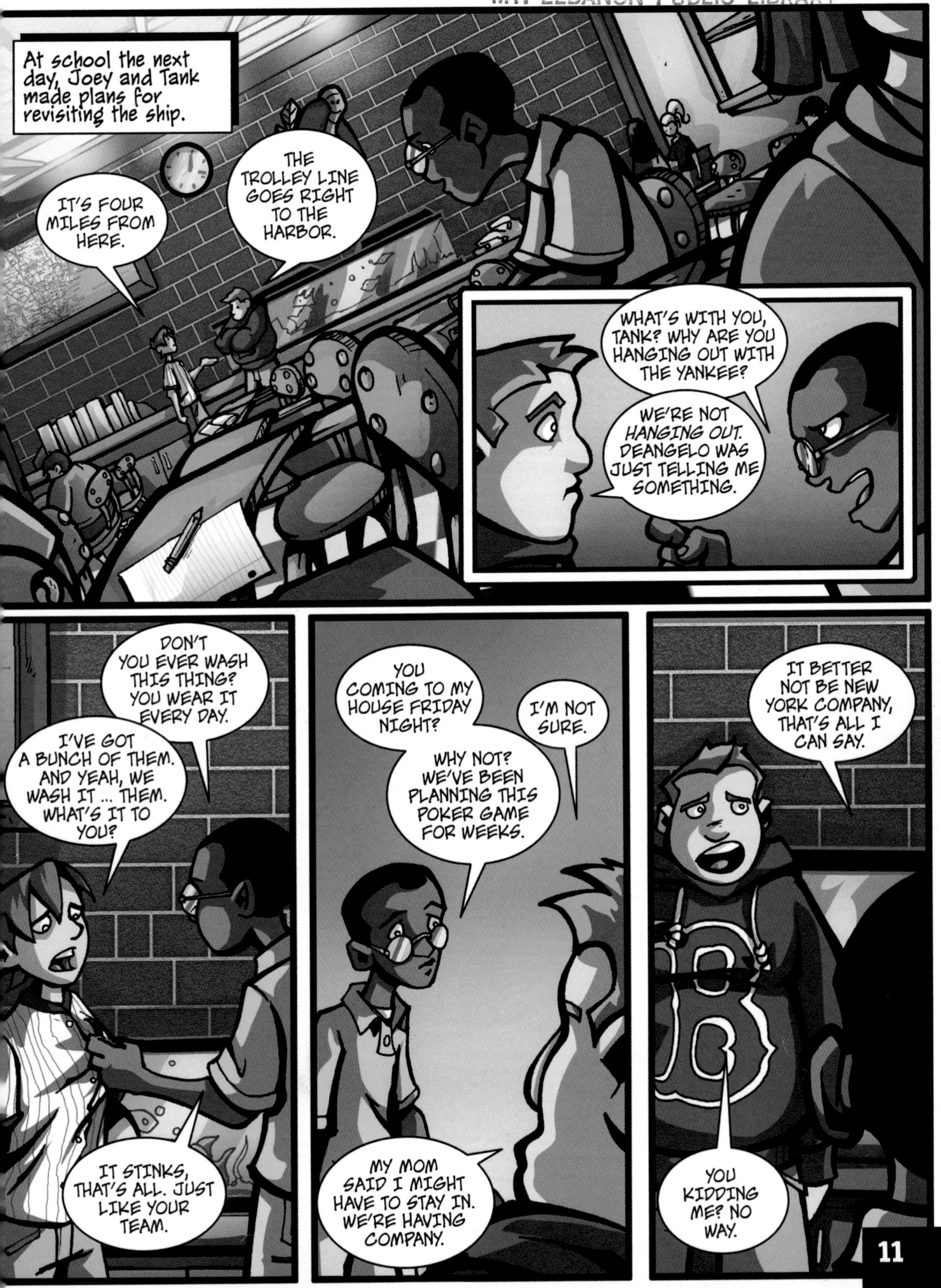
At school the next day, Joey and Tank made plans for revisiting the ship.
IT'S FOUR MILES FROM HERE.
THE TROLLEY LINE GOES RIGHT TO THE HARBOR.
WHAT'S WITH YOU, TANK? WHY ARE YOU HANGING OUT WITH THE YANKEE?
WE'RE NOT HANGING OUT. DEANGELO WAS JUST TELLING ME SOMETHING.
DON'T YOU EVER WASH THIS THING? YOU WEAR IT EVERY DAY.
I'VE GOT A BUNCH OF THEM. AND YEAH, WE WASH IT ... THEM. WHAT'S IT TO YOU?
IT STINKS, THAT'S ALL. JUST LIKE YOUR TEAM.
YOU COMING TO MY HOUSE FRIDAY NIGHT?
I'M NOT SURE.
WHY NOT? WE'VE BEEN PLANNING THIS POKER GAME FOR WEEKS.
MY MOM SAID I MIGHT HAVE TO STAY IN. WE'RE HAVING COMPANY.
IT BETTER NOT BE NEW YORK COMPANY, THAT'S ALL I CAN SAY.
YOU KIDDING ME? NO WAY.

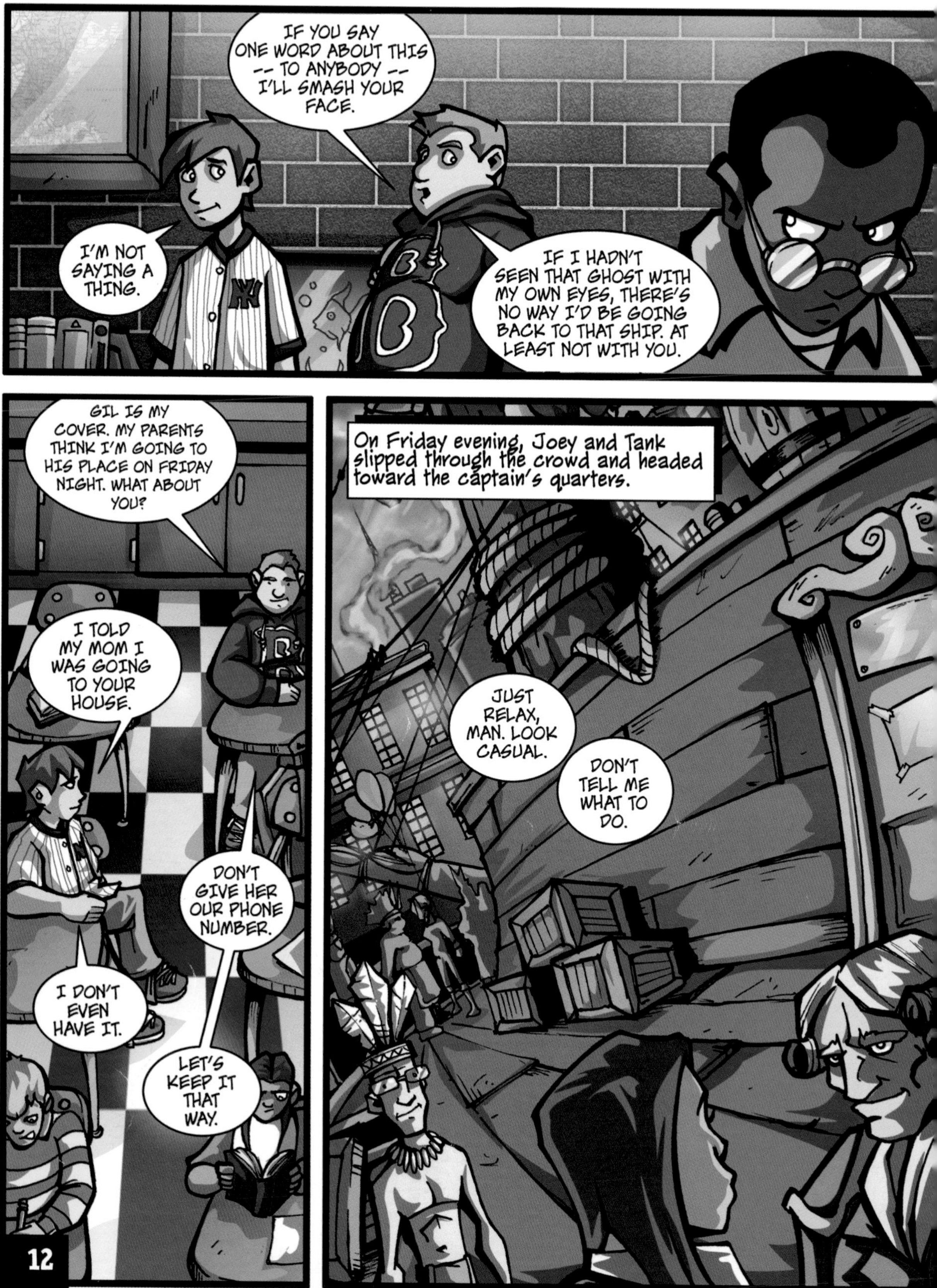
IF YOU SAY ONE WORD ABOUT THIS -- TO ANYBODY -- I'LL SMASH YOUR FACE.
I'M NOT SAYING A THING.
IF I HADN'T SEEN THAT GHOST WITH MY OWN EYES, THERE'S NO WAY I'D BE GOING BACK TO THAT SHIP. AT LEAST NOT WITH YOU.
GIL IS MY COVER. MY PARENTS THINK I'M GOING TO HIS PLACE ON FRIDAY NIGHT. WHAT ABOUT YOU?
I TOLD MY MOM I WAS GOING TO YOUR HOUSE.
DON'T GIVE HER OUR PHONE NUMBER.
I DON'T EVEN HAVE IT.
LET'S KEEP IT THAT WAY.
On Friday evening, Joey and Tank slipped through the crowd and headed toward the captain's quarters.
JUST RELAX, MAN. LOOK CASUAL.
DON'T TELL ME WHAT TO DO.

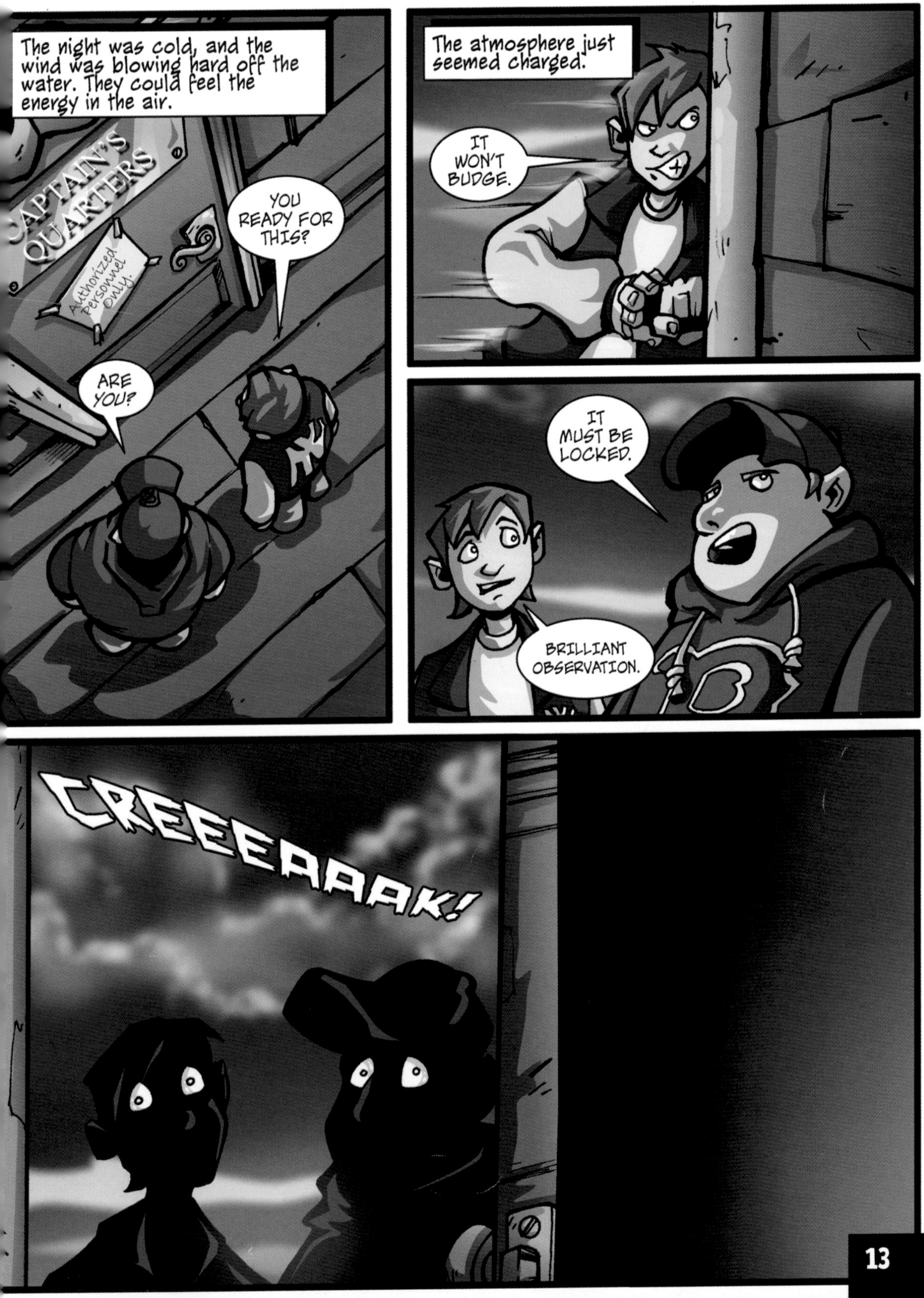
The night was cold, and the wind was blowing hard off the water. They could feel the energy in the air.
CAPTAIN'S QUARTERS
Authorized Personnel Only.
YOU READY FOR THIS?
ARE YOU?
The atmosphere just seemed charged.
IT WON'T BUDGE.
IT MUST BE LOCKED.
BRILLIANT OBSERVATION.
CREEEEAAAAK!

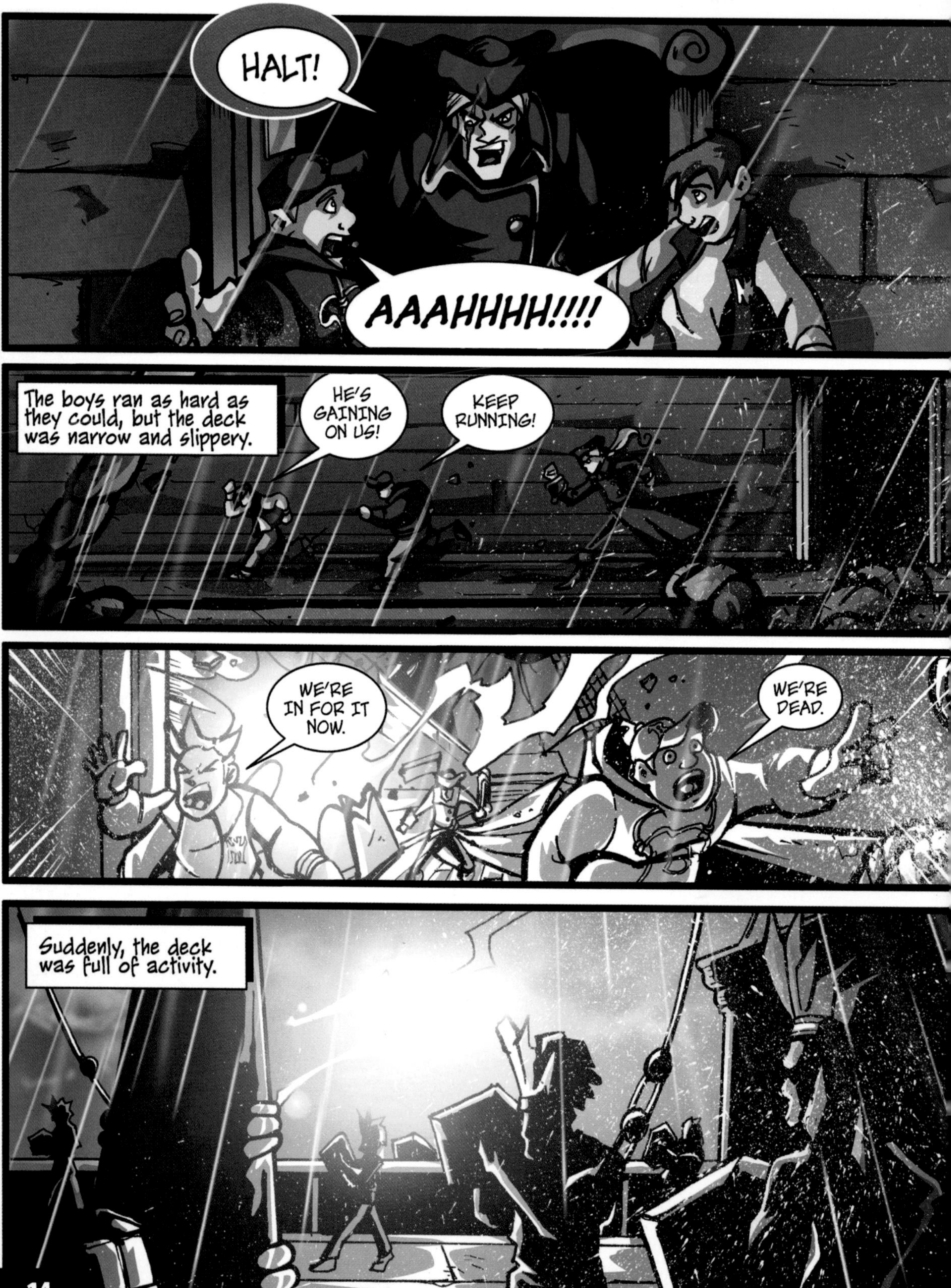
HALT!
AAAHHHH!!!!
The boys ran as hard as they could, but the deck was narrow and slippery.
HE'S GAINING ON US!
KEEP RUNNING!
WE'RE IN FOR IT NOW.
WE'RE DEAD.
Suddenly, the deck was full of activity.

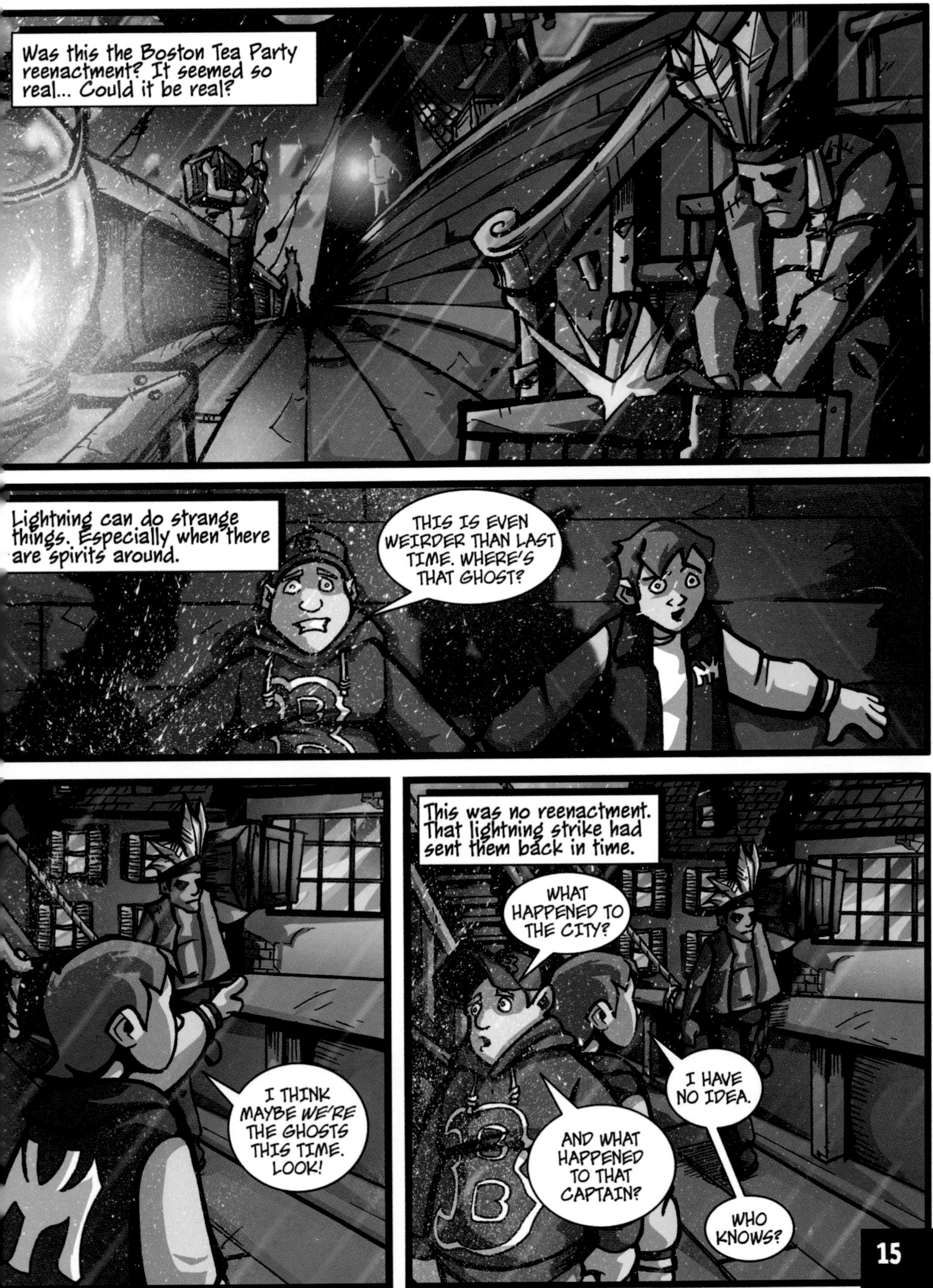
Was this the Boston Tea Party reenactment? It seemed so real... Could it be real?
Lightning can do strange things. Especially when there are spirits around.
THIS IS EVEN WEIRDER THAN LAST TIME. WHERE'S THAT GHOST?
I THINK MAYBE WE'RE THE GHOSTS THIS TIME. LOOK!
This was no reenactment. That lightning strike had sent them back in time.
WHAT HAPPENED TO THE CITY?
I HAVE NO IDEA.
AND WHAT HAPPENED TO THAT CAPTAIN?
WHO KNOWS?

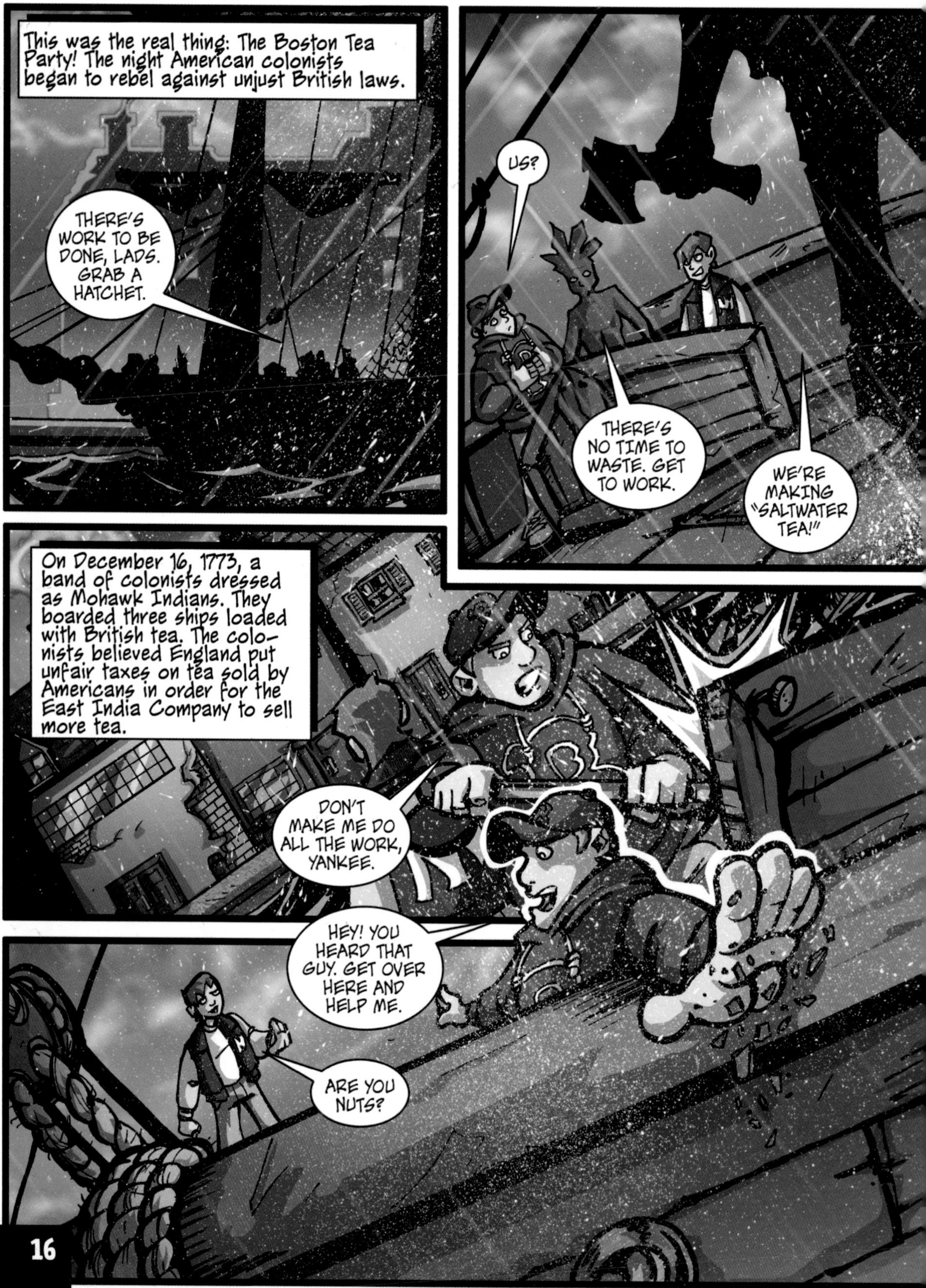
This was the real thing: The Boston Tea Party! The night American colonists began to rebel against unjust British laws.
THERE'S WORK TO BE DONE, LADS. GRAB A HATCHET.
US?
THERE'S NO TIME TO WASTE. GET TO WORK.
WE'RE MAKING "SALTWATER TEA!"
On December 16, 1773, a band of colonists dressed as Mohawk Indians. They boarded three ships loaded with British tea. The colonists believed England put unfair taxes on tea sold by Americans in order for the East India Company to sell more tea.
DON'T MAKE ME DO ALL THE WORK, YANKEE.
HEY! YOU HEARD THAT GUY. GET OVER HERE AND HELP ME.
ARE YOU NUTS?

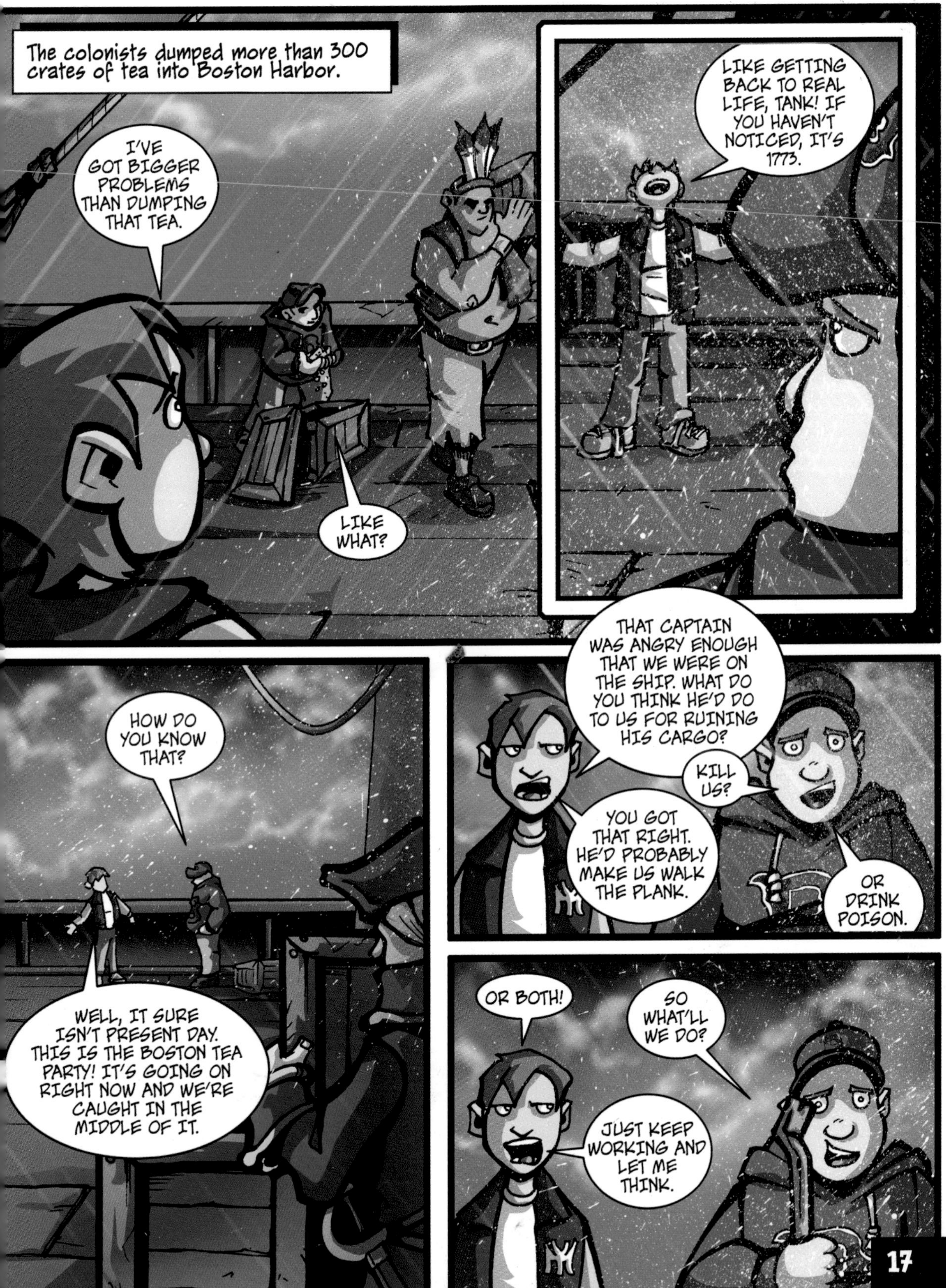
The colonists dumped more than 300 crates of tea into Boston Harbor.
I'VE GOT BIGGER PROBLEMS THAN DUMPING THAT TEA.
LIKE WHAT?
LIKE GETTING BACK TO REAL LIFE, TANK! IF YOU HAVEN'T NOTICED, IT'S 1773.
HOW DO YOU KNOW THAT?
WELL, IT SURE ISN'T PRESENT DAY. THIS IS THE BOSTON TEA PARTY! IT'S GOING ON RIGHT NOW AND WE'RE CAUGHT IN THE MIDDLE OF IT.
THAT CAPTAIN WAS ANGRY ENOUGH THAT WE WERE ON THE SHIP. WHAT DO YOU THINK HE'D DO TO US FOR RUINING HIS CARGO?
KILL US?
YOU GOT THAT RIGHT. HE'D PROBABLY MAKE US WALK THE PLANK.
OR DRINK POISON.
OR BOTH!
SO WHAT'LL WE DO?
JUST KEEP WORKING AND LET ME THINK.

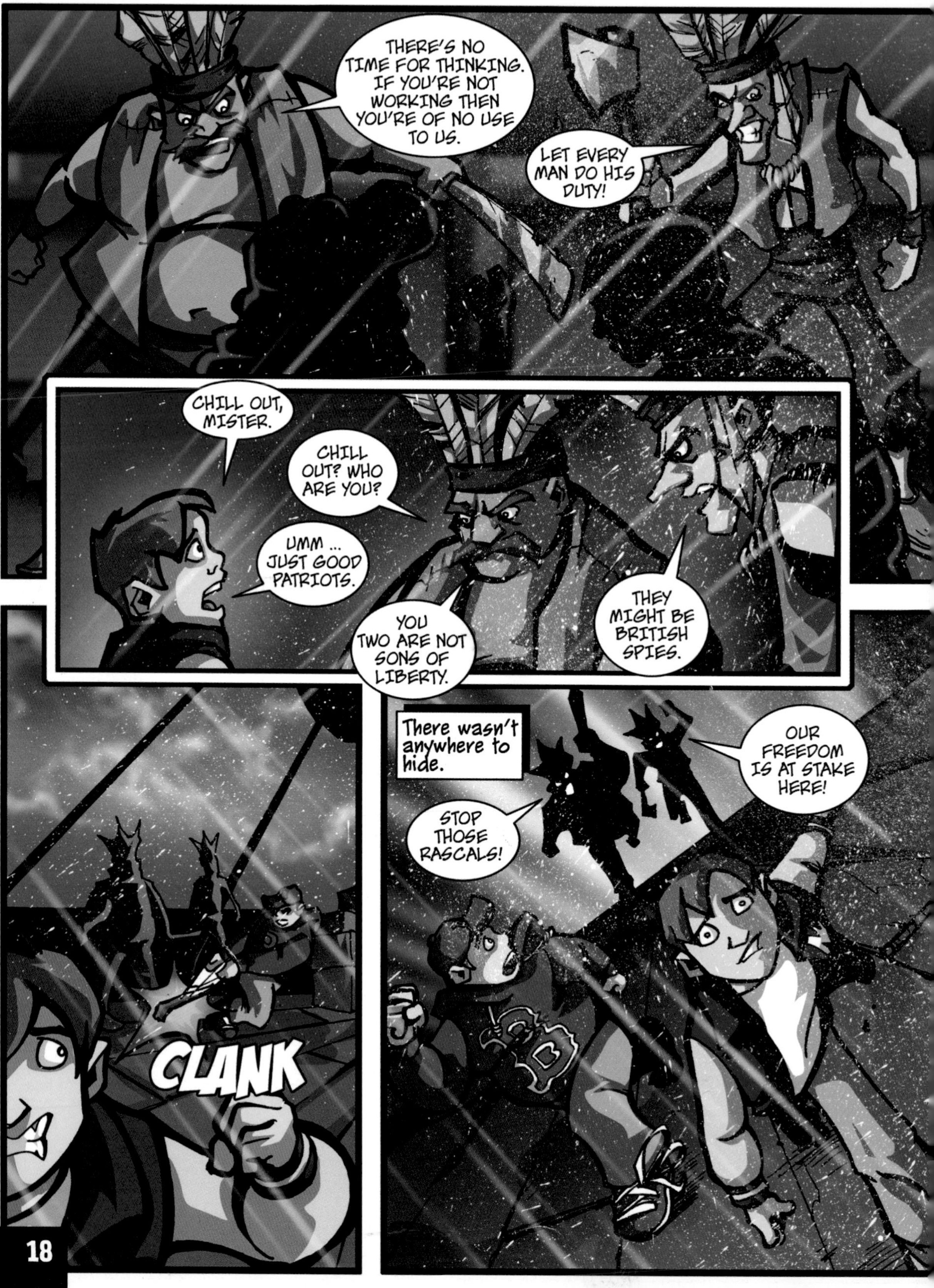

THERE'S NO TIME FOR THINKING. IF YOU'RE NOT WORKING THEN YOU'RE OF NO USE TO US.
LET EVERY MAN DO HIS DUTY!
CHILL OUT, MISTER.
CHILL OUT? WHO ARE YOU?
UMM ... JUST GOOD PATRIOTS.
YOU TWO ARE NOT SONS OF LIBERTY.
THEY MIGHT BE BRITISH SPIES.
CLANK
There wasn't anywhere to hide.
OUR FREEDOM IS AT STAKE HERE!
STOP THOSE RASCALS!

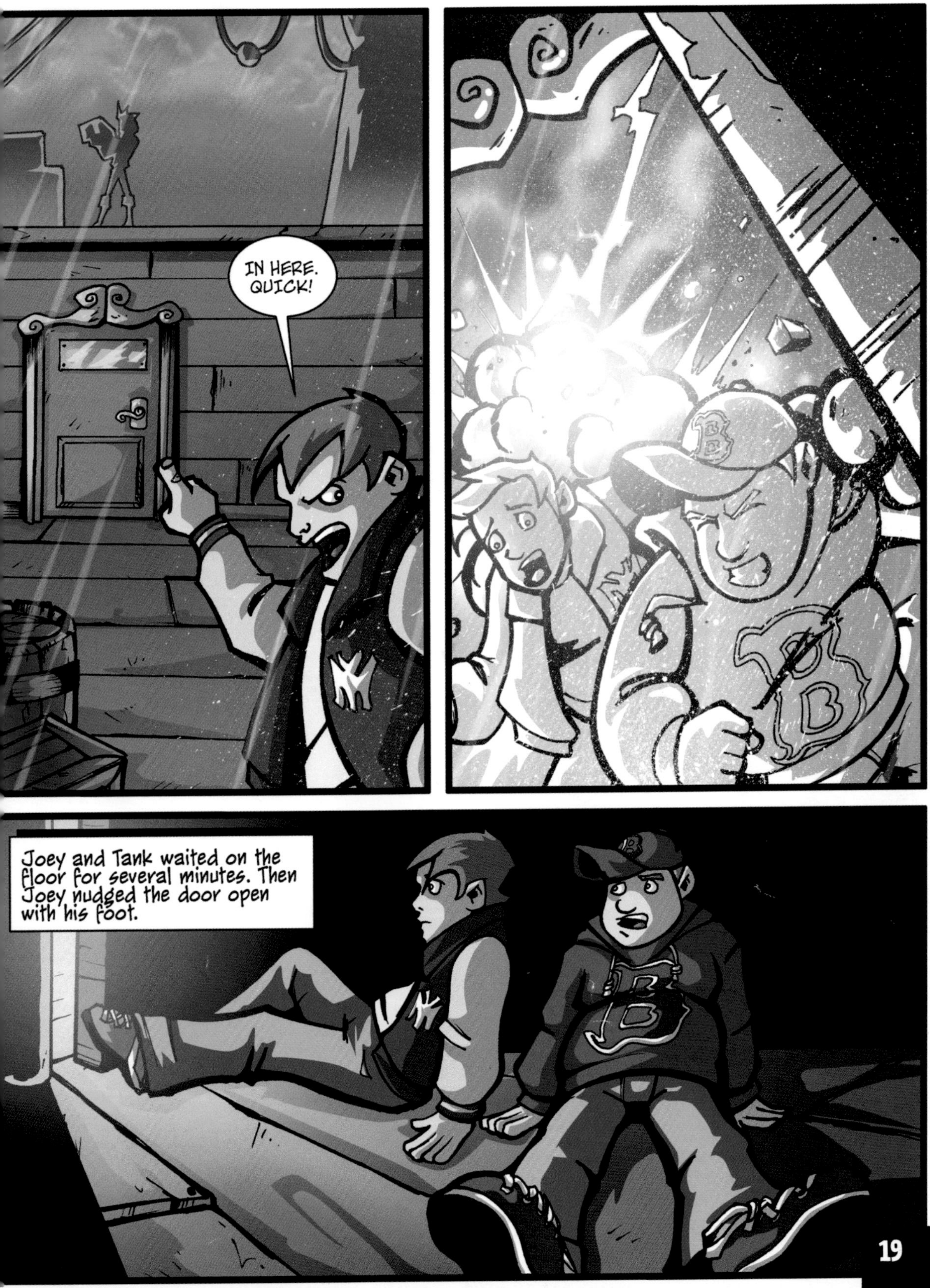
IN HERE. QUICK!
Joey and Tank waited on the floor for several minutes. Then Joey nudged the door open with his foot.

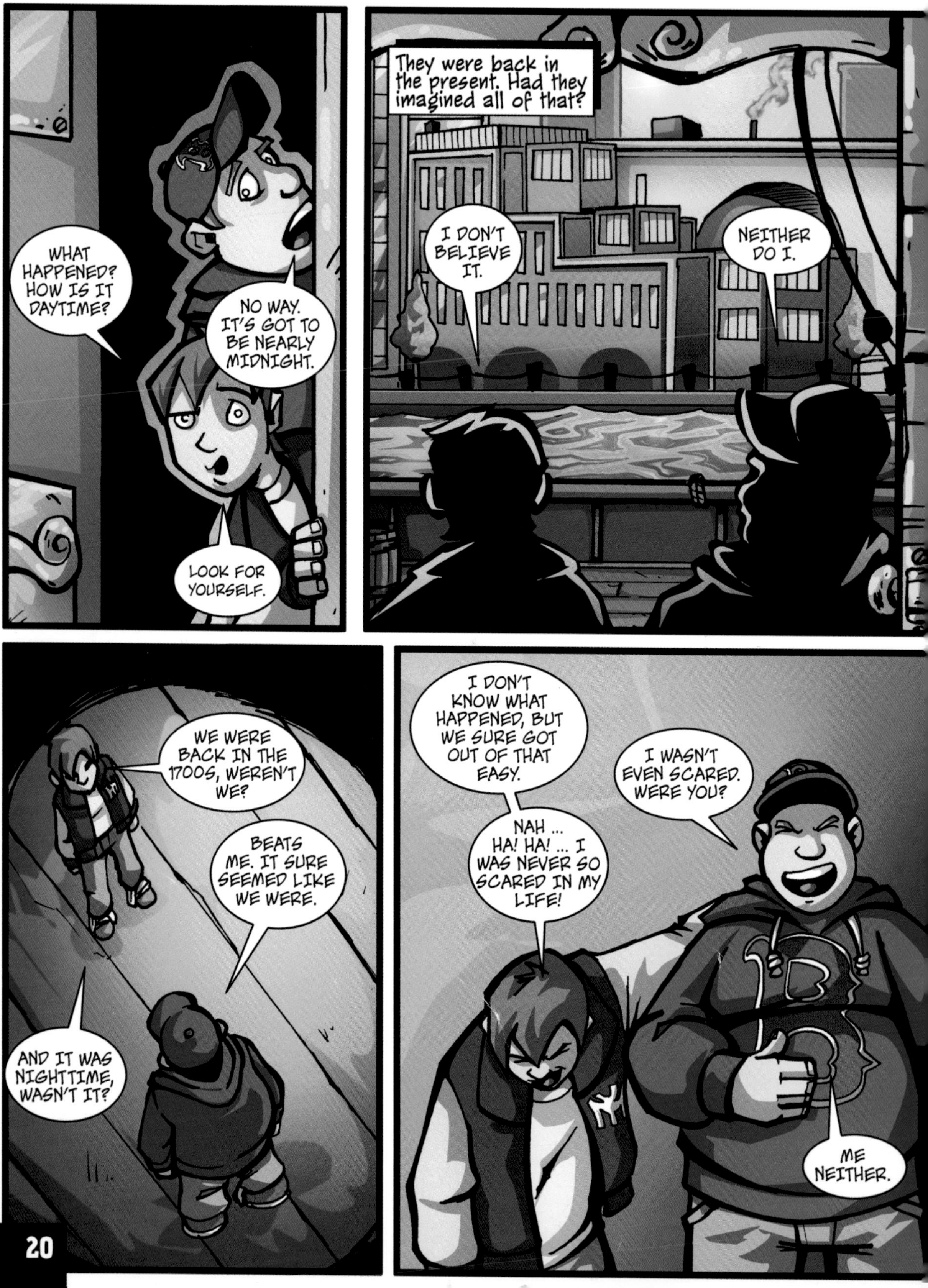
WHAT HAPPENED? HOW IS IT DAYTIME?
NO WAY. IT'S GOT TO BE NEARLY MIDNIGHT.
LOOK FOR YOURSELF.
They were back in the present. Had they imagined all of that?
I DON'T BELIEVE IT.
NEITHER DO I.
WE WERE BACK IN THE 1700S, WEREN'T WE?
BEATS ME. IT SURE SEEMED LIKE WE WERE.
AND IT WAS NIGHTTIME, WASN'T IT?
I DON'T KNOW WHAT HAPPENED, BUT WE SURE GOT OUT OF THAT EASY.
I WASN'T EVEN SCARED. WERE YOU?
NAH ... HA! HA! ... I WAS NEVER SO SCARED IN MY LIFE!
ME NEITHER.

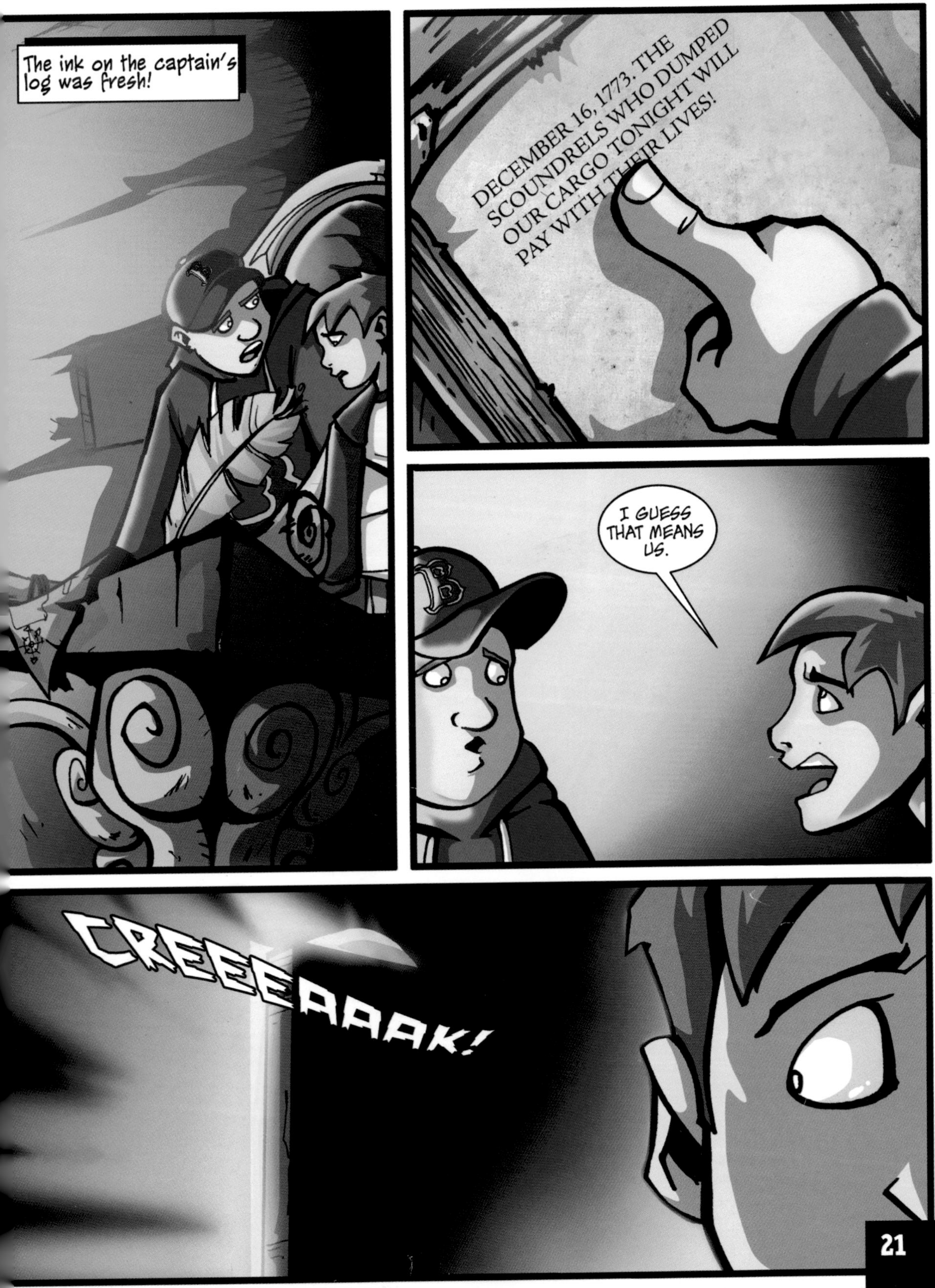
The ink on the captain's log was fresh!
DECEMBER 16, 1773. THE SCOUNDRELS WHO DUMPED OUR CARGO TONIGHT WILL PAY WITH THEIR LIVES!
I GUESS THAT MEANS US.
CREEEAAAK!

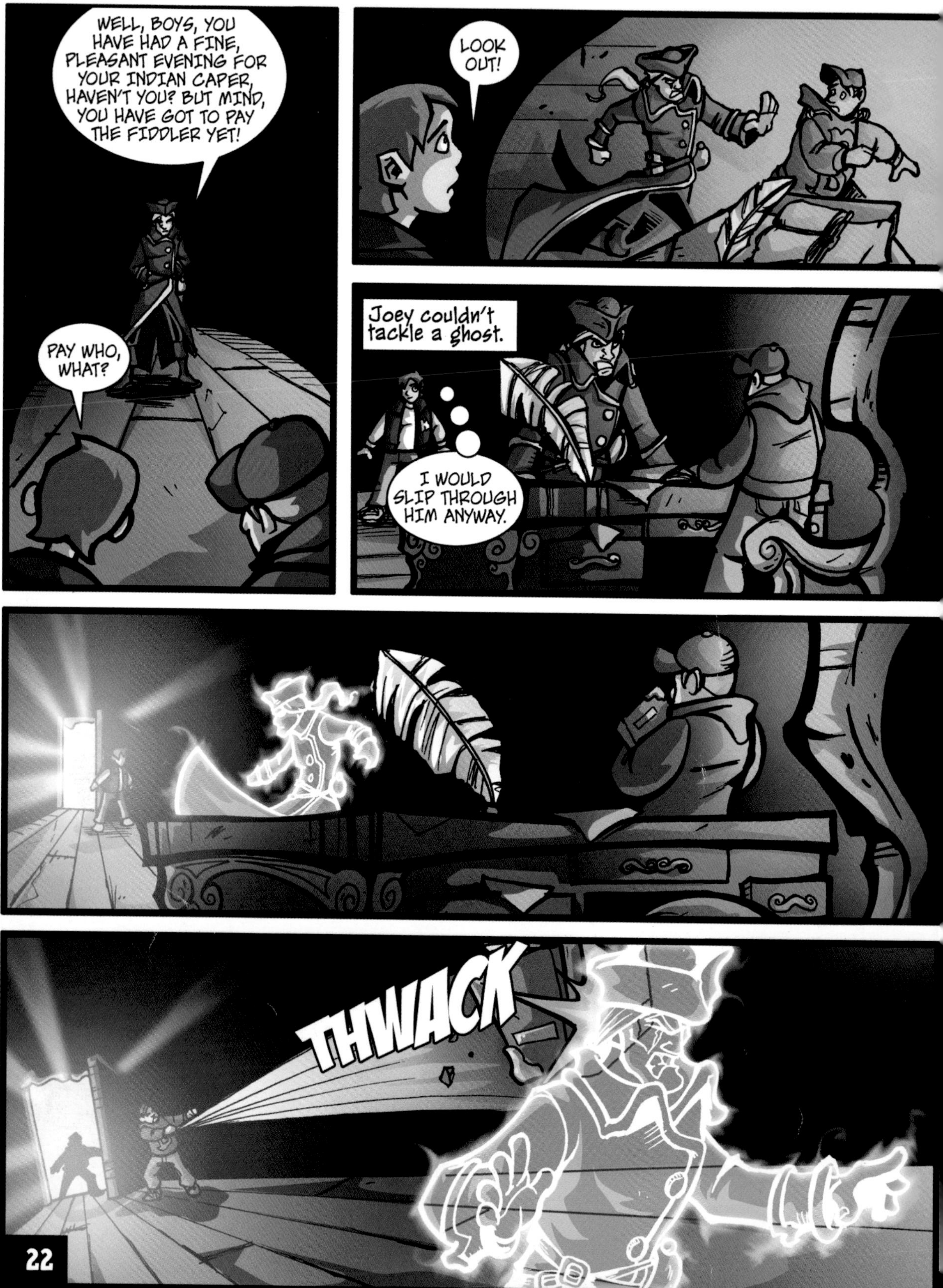
WELL, BOYS, YOU HAVE HAD A FINE, PLEASANT EVENING FOR YOUR INDIAN CAPER, HAVEN'T YOU? BUT MIND, YOU HAVE GOT TO PAY THE FIDDLER YET!
PAY WHO, WHAT?
LOOK OUT!
Joey couldn't tackle a ghost.
I WOULD SLIP THROUGH HIM ANYWAY.
THWACK

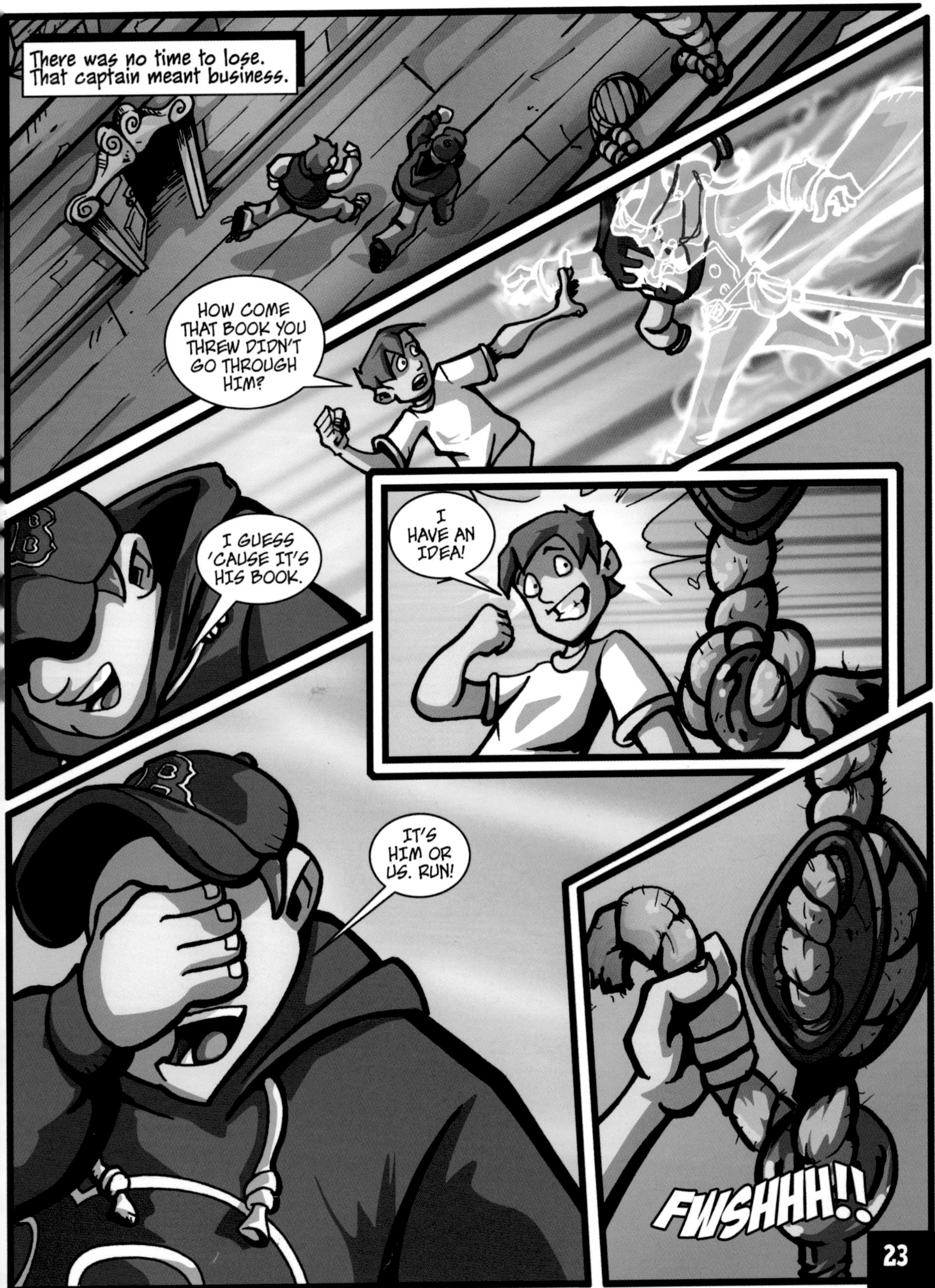
There was no time to lose. That captain meant business.
HOW COME THAT BOOK YOU THREW DIDN'T GO THROUGH HIM?
I GUESS 'CAUSE IT'S HIS BOOK.
I HAVE AN IDEA!
IT'S HIM OR US. RUN!
FWSHHH!!

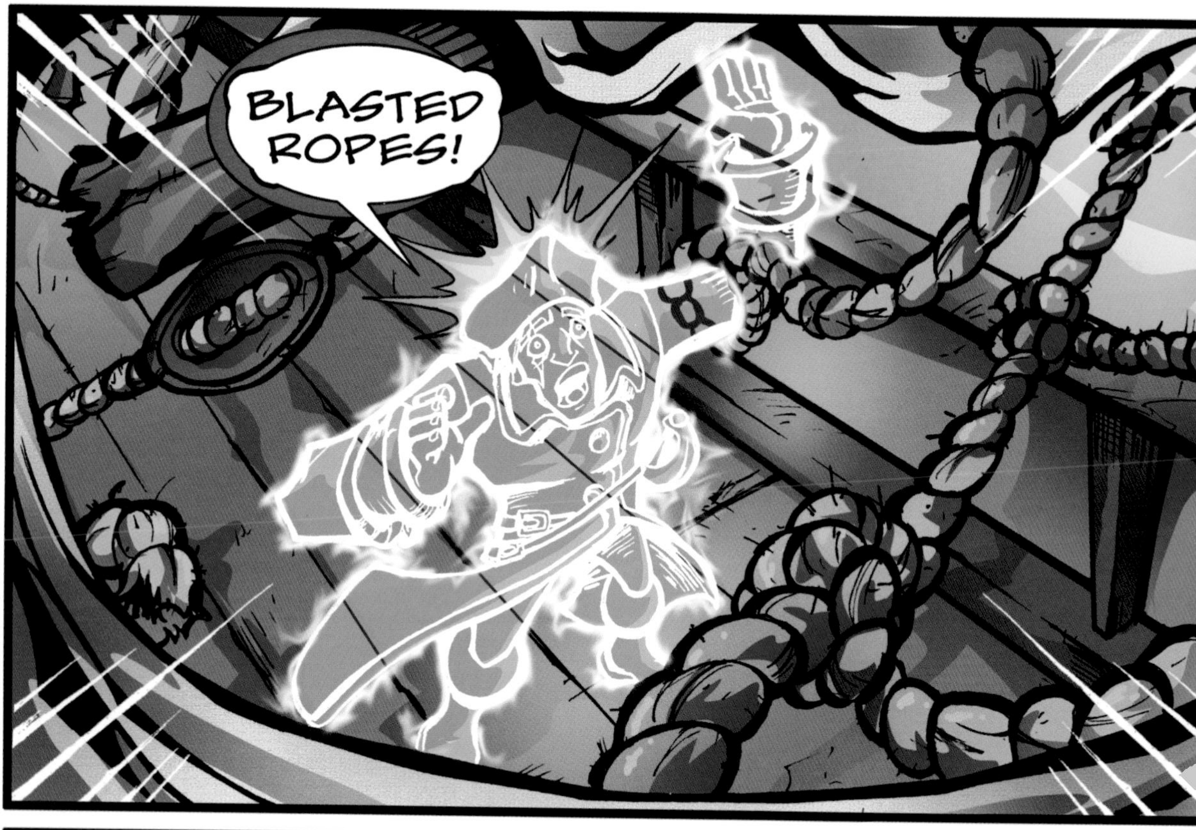
BLASTED ROPES!

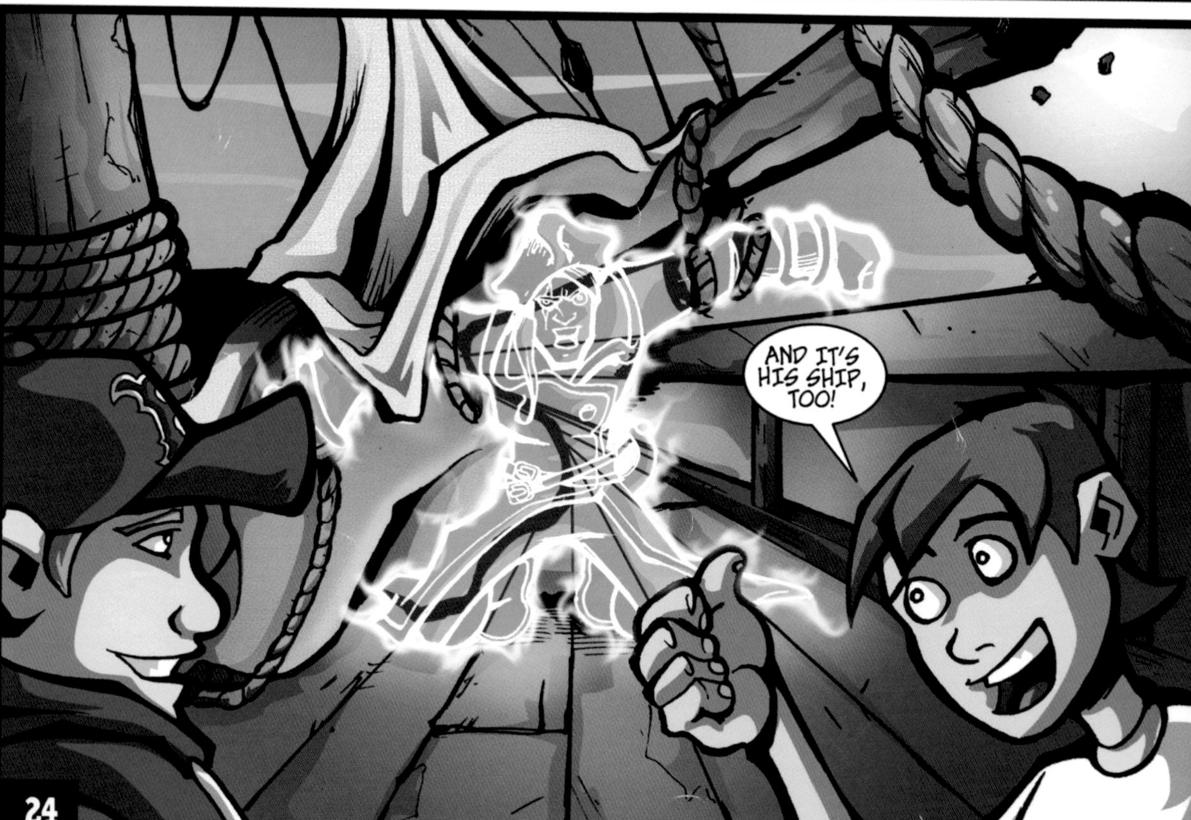
AND IT'S HIS SHIP, TOO!

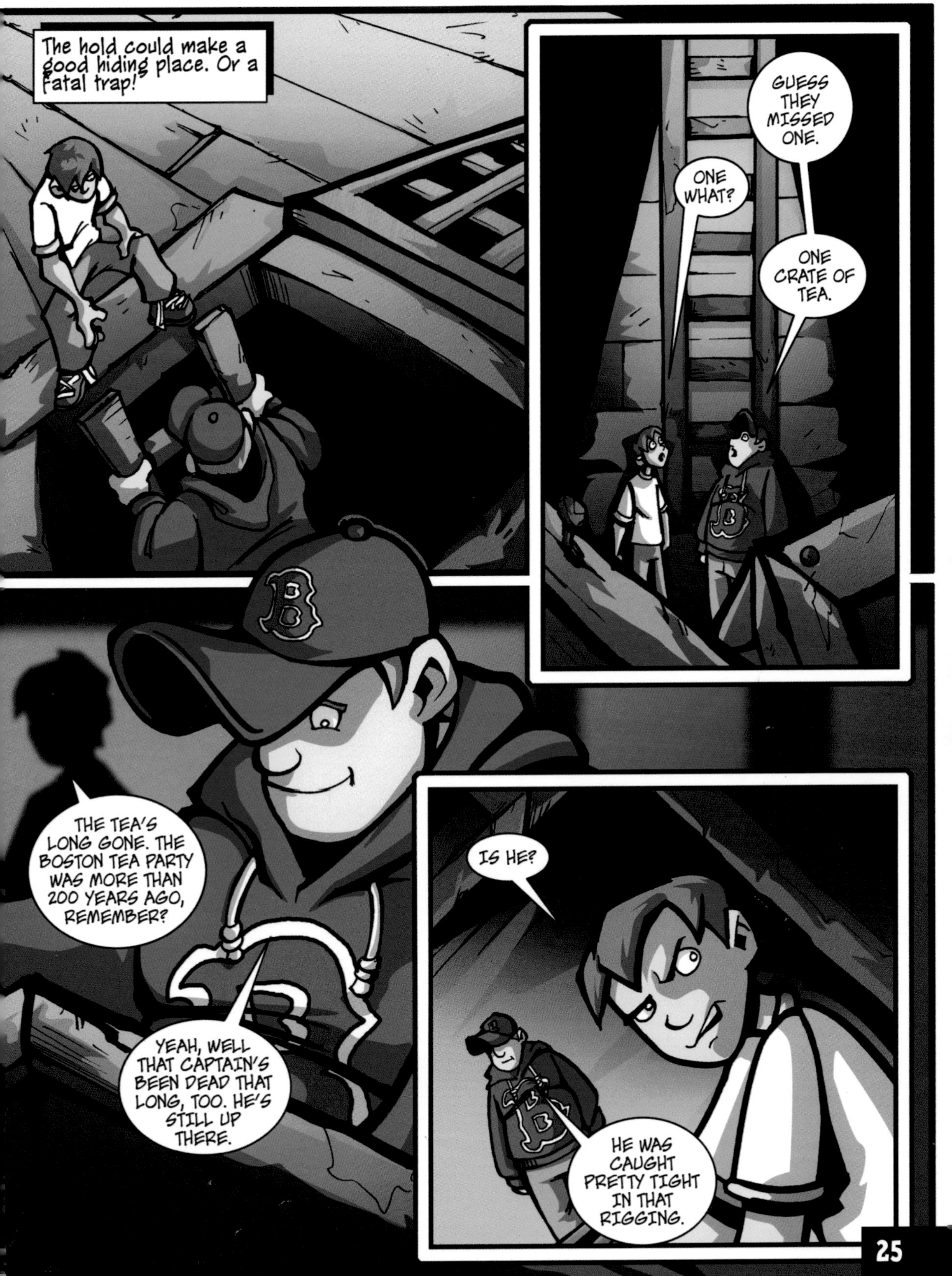

The hold could make a good hiding place. Or a fatal trap!
GUESS THEY MISSED ONE.
ONE WHAT?
ONE CRATE OF TEA.
THE TEA'S LONG GONE. THE BOSTON TEA PARTY WAS MORE THAN 200 YEARS AGO, REMEMBER?
YEAH, WELL THAT CAPTAIN'S BEEN DEAD THAT LONG, TOO. HE'S STILL UP THERE.
IS HE?
HE WAS CAUGHT PRETTY TIGHT IN THAT RIGGING.

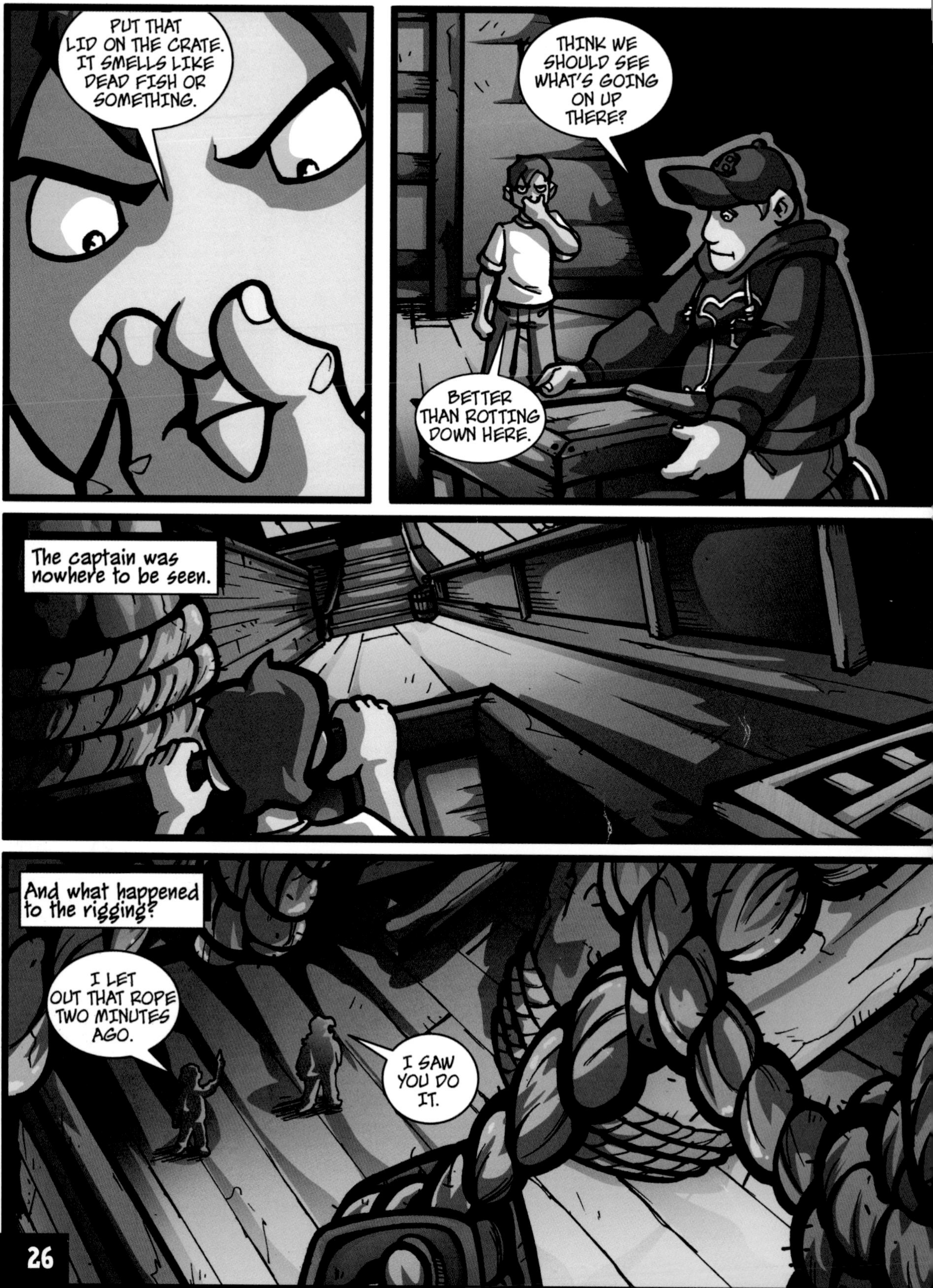
PUT THAT LID ON THE CRATE. IT SMELLS LIKE DEAD FISH OR SOMETHING.
THINK WE SHOULD SEE WHAT'S GOING ON UP THERE?
BETTER THAN ROTTING DOWN HERE.
The captain was nowhere to be seen.
And what happened to the rigging?
I LET OUT THAT ROPE TWO MINUTES AGO.
I SAW YOU DO IT.

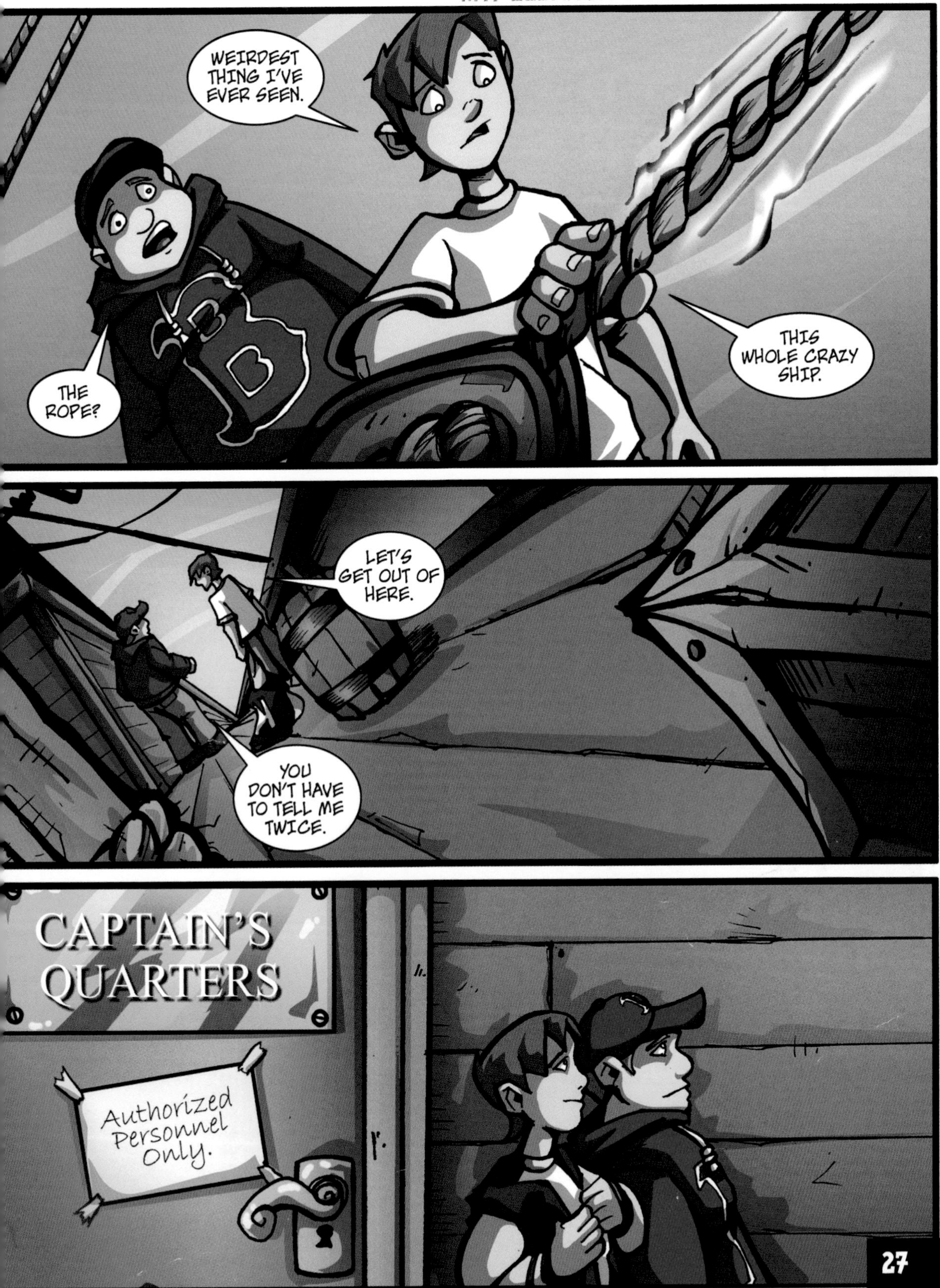
WEIRDEST THING I'VE EVER SEEN.
THE ROPE?
THIS WHOLE CRAZY SHIP.
LET'S GET OUT OF HERE.
YOU DON'T HAVE TO TELL ME TWICE.
CAPTAIN'S QUARTERS
Authorized Personnel Only.

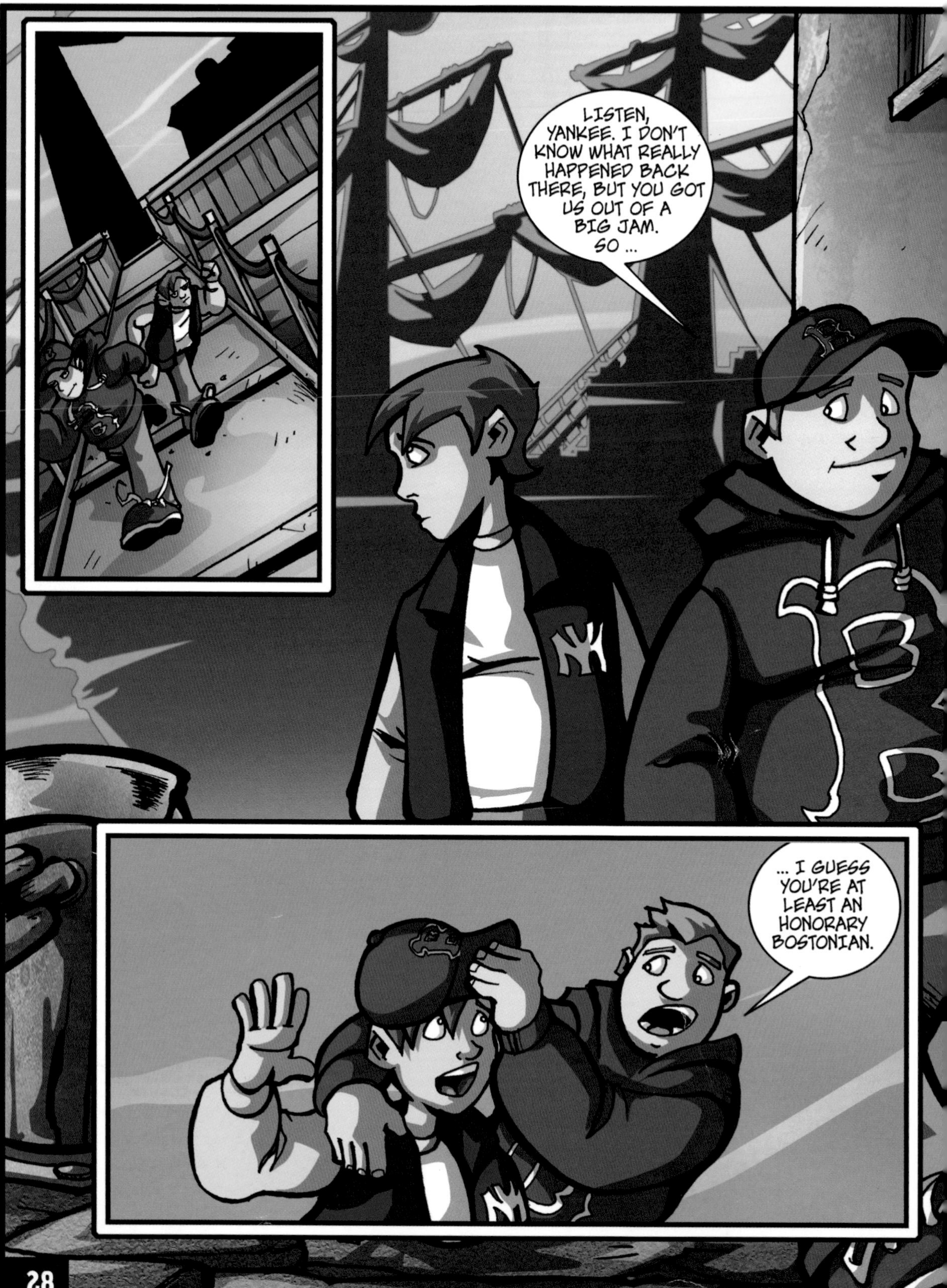
LISTEN, YANKEE. I DON'T KNOW WHAT REALLY HAPPENED BACK THERE, BUT YOU GOT US OUT OF A BIG JAM. SO ...
... I GUESS YOU'RE AT LEAST AN HONORARY BOSTONIAN.

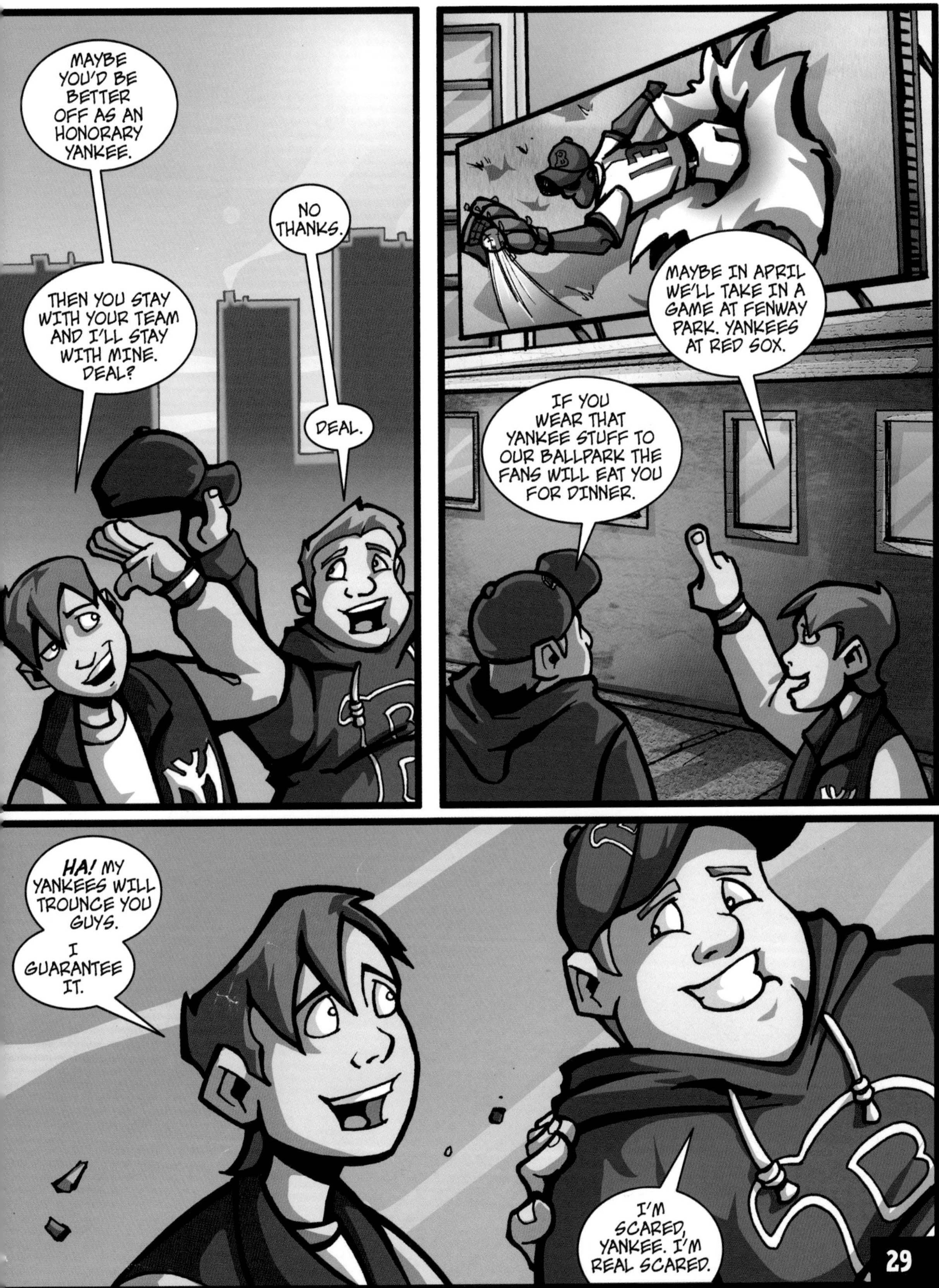
MAYBE YOU'D BE BETTER OFF AS AN HONORARY YANKEE.
NO THANKS.
THEN YOU STAY WITH YOUR TEAM AND I'LL STAY WITH MINE. DEAL?
DEAL.
MAYBE IN APRIL WE'LL TAKE IN A GAME AT FENWAY PARK. YANKEES AT RED SOX.
IF YOU WEAR THAT YANKEE STUFF TO OUR BALLPARK THE FANS WILL EAT YOU FOR DINNER.
HA! MY YANKEES WILL TROUNCE YOU GUYS.
I GUARANTEE IT.
I'M SCARED, YANKEE. I'M REAL SCARED.

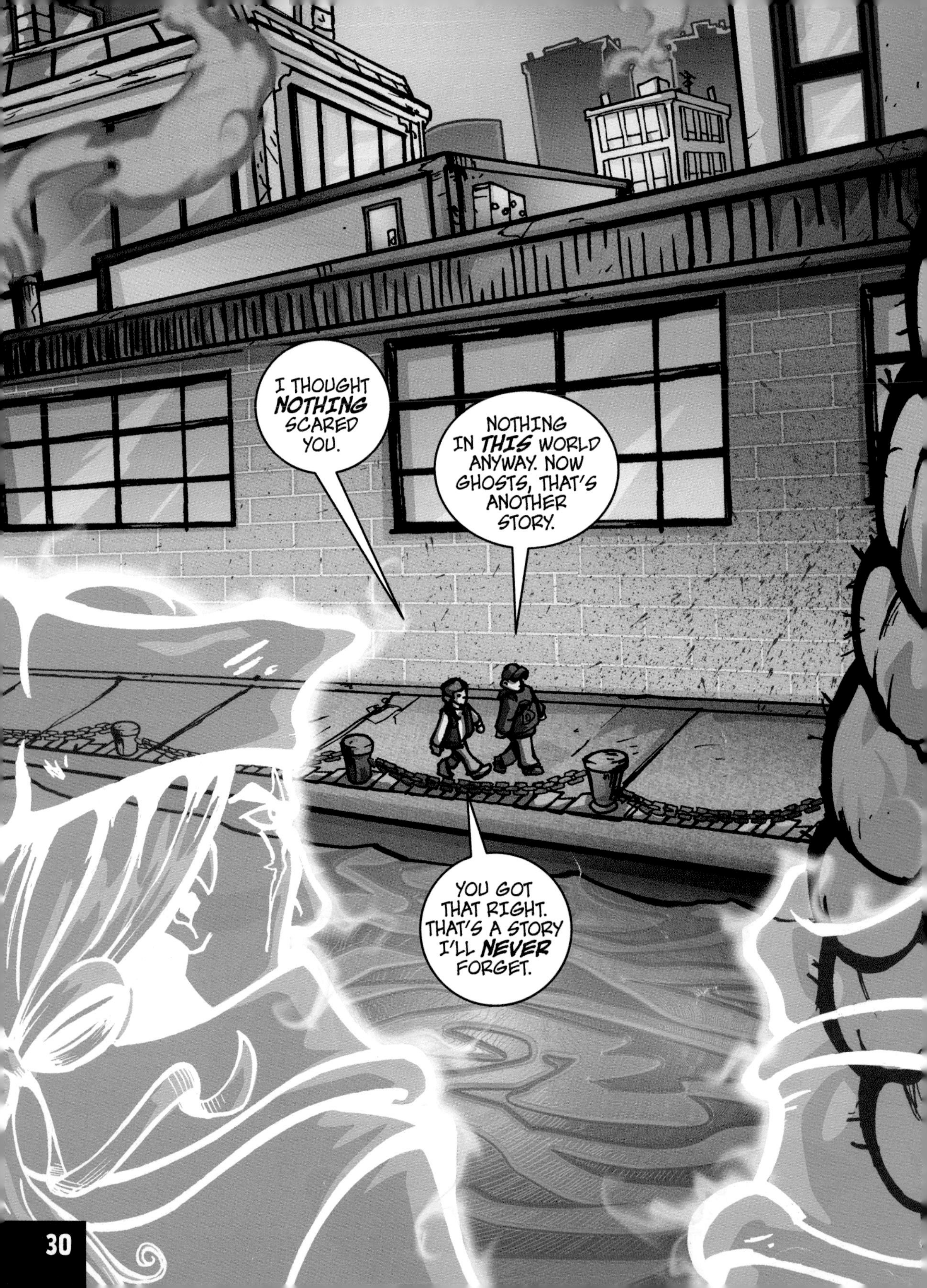
I THOUGHT NOTHING SCARED YOU.
NOTHING IN THIS WORLD ANYWAY. NOW GHOSTS, THAT'S ANOTHER STORY.
YOU GOT THAT RIGHT. THAT'S A STORY I'LL NEVER FORGET.

THE BOSTON TEA PARTY

On December 16, 1773, colonist Samuel Adams and a group of Patriots headed for Boston Harbor. Three ships were docked in the harbor, and each carried precious cargo: crates of British tea.

The colonists, known as the Sons of Liberty, were angry because the British government had recently passed the Tea Act. That law made the cost of imported British tea much cheaper than any that was imported by colonial merchants. The colonists rebelled because the government had created a British monopoly on tea, which was unfair to American importers.

Adams and the others demanded that the three ships in Boston Harbor return to England. When they refused, the Sons of Liberty launched what came to be known as the Boston Tea Party. It is considered a crucial act of the American Revolution.

That night, the colonists disguised themselves as Mohawk Indians. They boarded the ships and destroyed 342 crates of tea, dumping the cargo into the ocean. The ships included the *Dartmouth*, the *Eleanor*, and the *Beaver*.

It is said that British Admiral Montague, who had watched the Tea Party from nearby, yelled to the Patriots, "Well, boys, you have had a fine, pleasant evening for your Indian caper, haven't you? But mind, you have got to pay the fiddler yet!"

The British government issued even stricter laws on the colonists soon after. One of those acts closed the port of Boston. Within two years, the Revolutionary War was under way.

BOSTON TEA PARTY REENACTMENT 8 PM DECEMBER 16 ABOARD THE DARTMOUTH

GLOSSARY

afoot – in the process of happening.

atmosphere – a feeling or influence surrounding an area.

Bronx – a neighborhood in New York City.

lunge – a sudden forward reach for something.

reenactment – a performance of an event that had happened in the past.

rigging – the ropes and chains used to work a ship's sails.

swab – a sailor.

trounce – to defeat by a large number of points.

WEB SITES

To learn more about the *Dartmouth*, visit ABDO Group online at **www.abdopublishing.com.** Web sites about the ship are featured on our Book Links page. These links are routinely monitored and updated to provide the most current information available.